Vanishing Act

Murder by Misdirection 2

Debra Snow

MIND BENDER PRESS

Copyright 2020 Debra Snow

This is a work of fiction. Names, characters, places, and incidents either are the product of the author's imagination or are used fictitiously. Any resemblance to actual persons, living or dead, events, or locales is entirely coincidental.

All rights reserved. No part of this publication may be reproduced, stored in a retrieval system, or transmitted in any form or by any means, electronic, mechanical, photocopying, recording, or otherwise, without the prior written permission of the publisher, except in the case of brief quotations embodied in critical reviews and certain other noncommercial uses permitted by copyright law. For permission requests, write to the publisher at the address below.

Cover Design: Marianne Nowicki, PremadeEbookCoverShop.com
Editing: Brandi Aquino; www.editingdonewrite.com

ISBN-10: 173422911X
ISBN-13: 978-1734229110

Published by:
Mindbender Press
474 South Main Street
Phillipsburg NJ 08865
www.mindbenderpress.com

Books From Mindbender Press

PARANORMAL MYSTERY:
(In The Mind Series)
FIRE IN THE MIND
SEDUCTION IN THE MIND
REUNION IN THE MIND
HAUNTED IN THE MIND
DEVOTION IN THE MIND
ASYLUM IN THE MIND
SPECTER IN THE MIND
VENGEANCE IN THE MIND
ECHOES IN THE MIND

HORROR:
THE MUSE: *A Novel Of Unrelenting Terror*
KEPT IN THE DARK
THE VANISHING

ULTIMATE URBAN FANTASY:
THE WIZARDS OF CENTRAL PARK WEST
THE VAMPIRES OF GREENWICH VILLAGE

ROMANTIC MYSTERY:
A STUDY IN MURDER
MURDER BY MISDIRECTION
VANISHING ACT

1. Flash Appearance --------------------------------- 1
2. Bill In Lemon ----------------------------------- 23
3. Card Through Window --------------------------- 35
4. Book Of The Mind -------------------------------- 47
5. Inexhaustible Bottle ----------------------------- 59
6. Asrah Levitation -------------------------------- 69
7. Banana-Bandada --------------------------------- 83
8. Dagger Head Box -------------------------------- 95
9. Brainwave Deck -------------------------------- 107
10. Penetration Pen ------------------------------- 117
11. Square Circle --------------------------------- 129
12. Assistant's Revenge --------------------------- 141
13. Aztec Lady ----------------------------------- 155
14. Quick Change --------------------------------- 165
15. The Four Burglars ---------------------------- 177
16. Devil's Torture Chamber ---------------------- 187
17. Bullet Catch ---------------------------------- 201
18. Thumb Tip ----------------------------------- 215
19. Elmsly Count --------------------------------- 229
20. Magic Coloring Book -------------------------- 241
About The Author -------------------------------- 261

Dedication

To my parents,
George & Viola Snow
who always encouraged me
to walk my own path

Love is the magician that pulls man out of his own hat.

—Ben Hecht

You don't get into magic. Magic gets into you.
—David Blaine

Foreword

Writing is always a fun experience for me, and I hope you enjoy my books as much as I enjoy creating them.

It is amazing to me that so many of my plots and my husband's, Arjay Lewis, revolve around writers and writing. Since this novel touched on using books to push drugs, it gave me a chance to poke a little fun at both my husband and my publisher. I made the villainous publisher "Brain Bender Press" which is a direct spoof of "Mindbender Press" our own publisher.

I also included several of my husband's real and make-believe books. His most popular novel is "*THE MUSE*" a horror novel which has won 14 awards. I referred to it by name, and also several non-existent tomes mentioned within *that* book. (Which, of course, features writers as both the villain and the hero.)

There is a little less magic in this mystery, unlike *Murder By Misdirection*, but I did like the way it worked out. The third book in the trilogy *Under No Illusion* should be out in the fall.

Debra Snow
January 2020

1. Flash Appearance

Prophecy Thompson pushed her way through the front door of the four-story brownstone. It had been a tough day, with two homicides in a three block radius.

She was a tall woman of mixed race, her mother African-American and her father Caucasian, which gave her skin a warm caramel hue, but her eyes were a strong blue. The dark suit jacket of her pantsuit hid her service weapon, but Prophecy could feel the reassuring weight of it as she strode down the hall.

A uniformed policewoman gestured to her from a doorway. "Here, detective," said the auburn-haired woman. She wore her long hair in a ponytail that went down her back, and her hat was pulled to just above her blue eyes. She stood aside as Prophecy approached to allow the detective in.

Prophecy halted next to her, giving a quick look around to make sure no one was close. "Hey, Julie, how are you holding up?"

"Good, Pro," Julie said, also glancing to make sure they were alone. It was frowned on for a uniformed officer and a detective to refer to each other by their first names. "How was the other crime scene?"

"Rough, lots of blood," Pro responded. "Your boyfriend will be here soon. How are the two of you doing?"

Julie Barker gave another peek down the hallway. She lowered her voice and said excitedly, "Pro, I think Tom is going to pop the question!"

Pro's eyes widened. "Really?"

Julie nodded excitedly. "I think so. He's been dropping hints."

"Well, I'm all for it. You are just what my partner needs."

"You think so?" Julie fretted.

"Oh yeah, lady, you know it." Pro glanced over and saw that Barker's partner, Bailey, was approaching. He was taller than his partner, but Pro still had an inch on him with her six-foot-tall frame. Bailey was a well-muscled man, older than both the ladies, and with a bald head with a fringe of brown hair on the sides. Fortunately, with his hat on, only his hair was visible. "Thank you, Barker," Pro said and stepped into the room. "Officer Bailey, please bring me up to speed."

"Of course, detective, follow me," Bailey said, and they made their way through the small living room and into the tiny bedroom.

There, a body lay on the floor.

Pro scanned the room with the eyes of a practiced detective and knelt next to the prone woman on the floor. From what Pro could see, she was in her forties, maybe fifty. She had dyed her hair, making it a dark brown that did not look natural. She was dressed in sweats and socks, but with no shoes. She lay on the floor, her head and neck at an unnatural angle, and her brown eyes staring into oblivion.

She slipped on a latex glove from her pocket and spoke to Bailey. "Who found her?"

"Neighbor from across the hall. They were supposed to go running together. When the vic didn't answer the door or her phone, the neighbor came in with a spare key the vic gave her."

Pro pulled on the other glove. "Do we have an ID?"

"Neighbor says her name was May Johnson. I didn't go through the purse or anything because I know how much you like to do that, detective." Bailey smirked.

"Where is the neighbor now?"

"Across the hall in 1-F."

"Thanks, Bailey," Pro said and rose to stand up and look down at the corpse. "Did you see any entry point for an attacker?"

"Window in the bathroom is open, but it's got bars." Bailey shrugged. "I think she just fell and hit her head to put her neck at that weird angle. If anyone got in here, they'd haveta use a trapdoor."

"My father would be a better judge of that than me," Pro countered.

"Yeah, he was great with that outdoor magic show he did at the Fourth of July picnic this summer. It was nice of him to do that."

"It was the least he could do after the trouble he put our precinct through," Pro muttered.

"How's your old man doin' since he moved to NYC?"

She shook her head, annoyed. "Doing occasional events for private clients and dating my mom. I'm afraid to visit these days, in case they're getting romantic."

"Well, I'll secure the hall and watch for Detective Chu," Bailey said and moved away.

"Thanks, Bailey."

Pro stood in the room looking around. The bedroom was indeed small, even by New York standards, with furniture crammed in: a queen-sized bed and a bedside table took up most of the floor space currently unoccupied by Ms. Johnson's body. There were two bookcases built into opposite walls filled with novels and knickknacks.

She stepped into the bathroom where the window was indeed open. Since it was September, the air was still warm, and it was not uncommon to open a window in New York. She noted it was fairly new, quite large, and someone could easily climb in or out through it and into the first-floor apartment.

However, Bailey had been right; a set of metal window bars were on the outside of the building. There was a large hasp on the inside with a huge lock in place. Pro imagined that this would allow the resident to open the window in the event of a fire, provided they had the key for the lock. She wondered if the lock could be opened from the outside, but a metal plate welded to the frame blocked someone outside from reaching in.

She touched the cold metal, which was covered in layers of shiny black paint. The bars looked fairly new for this old brownstone. Just to be sure it was solid, she pulled on the lock, but there was no "give." This very much eliminated the possibility of someone getting into the apartment that way.

She opened the medicine cabinet and began to look at the contents. She thought about what an invasion this would be if someone began to go through her stuff, but that was what happened when someone died; all of their privacy was lost.

Pro looked over the contents on the little glass shelves: some makeup, lipstick and nail polish; several prescription drugs in brown plastic bottles, and an additional bottle that looked like it was for medicine but bore no label.

She picked up the prescriptions first. One for hormone replacement, but the others were painkillers—mostly opioids—and Pro frowned. It was hard to believe that one person could have several prescriptions for such drugs since they had become popular as a street drug in recent years.

She picked up the unlabeled bottle and opened it. In it was a powder that Pro guessed might be ground-up opioid tablets. This was the way opioids were sold on the street, made into a powder that could be snorted.

She resealed the bottle and closed the cabinet. She would have to wait for a ME and a toxicology report, but this probably was not a homicide, just a simple drug overdose.

She returned to the little bedroom again and looked down at May Johnson where she lay. This explained the unnatural position of the neck; the deceased could have fallen in the bedroom, probably hit her head on one of the bookcase shelves as she fell, just like Bailey had surmised.

She stepped gingerly over the body and into the living area just as her senior partner, Tom Chu, walked into the room. Tom was a first-generation American of Korean descent and was not as tall as Pro. He was thin, with the body of a dancer, but Pro had seen him use martial arts to take down much larger men when necessary. He was in his early thirties and was a great mentor and partner, as he never talked down to Pro or belittled her.

"Hey, partner," Pro said as he approached. "Any luck with the knife victim? Did you find the murder weapon?"

Tom gave a tight smile, which made his narrow eyes squint a bit. "No, but it could be there. Arterial spray from the knife across his throat, so you can't take two steps without walking into a pool of blood. Forensics is there now. What do we have here?"

"I have to admit, it looks like an overdose." Pro sighed and pulled out her notebook to scribble a few things as she spoke. "A collection of pain-killers in her medicine cabinet, maybe some street drugs."

"At least we caught an easy one. We'll be working that knife case for the next week," Tom worried.

"Did you complete the interview with the neighbor at the other scene?"

"The one who called 911? Yeah, I finished talking to him. Sorry you had to take off to catch this one."

"We were close-by; it made sense. Besides, that vic's apartment was similar to this one."

"Similar?" Chu questioned. "What do you mean?"

She focused her blue eyes on her partner. "Both places were brownstones, and both deaths were in first-floor apartments."

Tom couldn't help but smile. "I missed those details."

"That's because all you see is Julie Barker," Pro teased in a low voice.

Tom shot a quick look to the door and moved in closer to talk as quietly as he could. "Yeah, about that, Pro. I don't know what to do."

"What do you mean? She's great and crazy about you."

"But she's not Korean," Tom lamented. "My parents are old-fashioned that way. They want me to be with a Korean girl. They keep trying to set me up."

"Well, this is an easy one, Tom. What do you want?"

Her partner flushed deep red, and Pro fought not to smile. It was seldom that her tough-as-nails partner got flustered.

"I...um...want to marry her," Chu admitted.

"Then ask her! I know for a fact she'll say 'yes.'"

"Really?" Tom gulped.

"Definitely," Pro assured. "Now let's go through this place before forensics gets here. According to Bailey, the neighbor in 1-F found the body."

Tom nodded, regaining control. "We'll need to set up an interview with her."

"Good, let's go over the scene. I'll go through her purse."

The two homicide cops separated and went to their specific tasks. Pro went for the purse on the nearby table, while Chu examined the bookcase in the bedroom.

"I said you can't go in there, sir," Barker's high voice yelled as a man appeared in the apartment doorway. He was short and a bit overweight and dressed in jeans and work boots with a hastily buttoned red flannel shirt that was not tucked into the waist, so it hung over his trousers.

Both Chu and Pro stepped to the door to restrain the man. Since the apartment was small, it only took a couple of steps for both of them.

Pro raised her hands to stop the stranger, but it wasn't necessary. He stopped as soon as he saw the two detectives.

"Is she okay? Any damage to the place?" he bellowed with a thick New York accent.

"You can't come in here, sir," Chu ordered.

"The hell I can't! I'm the super!" he responded. "I gotta see if dere's any damage."

"Not until our team has gone through the room," Pro said and rose to her full six-foot height to tower over the little, plump man.

The man eyed Pro with a combination of fear and lust. "Whoa! You're a cop?"

"No, I'm a detective," she stormed. "Now, step into the hall so I don't have to cuff you!"

The man backed up, his hands raised. "Uh...okay, lady...I mean, officer...I mean, detective."

Once in the hall, Pro gave a nod to Chu who went back to examining the room and the remains of May Johnson. She also gave Barker a nod because she was nervous about the man pushing past her.

Pro turned to the flannel-wrapped man. "Okay, let's start over. You're the superintendent, the building manager. You got a name?"

"Uh...Manny."

"Last name?" Pro insisted as she drew out her notebook.

"Um...Schwartz. You got ID?"

Pro raised her eyes to stare at the superintendent. She pulled her shield from where it hung on the belt at her waist and held it out to the man.

"Okay, I guess that's legit."

"So glad you approve," Pro sniped. "Now, this apartment is off-limits until you are informed otherwise by the NYPD."

"Hey it's my job to keep the place looking good. We put a lot of renovations in that apartment recently."

"Is that so?" Pro said as she wrote in her pad.

"So, is the Johnson lady dead?"

"I ask the questions, please," Pro said and peered at him.

"Whoa, I ain't never seen a black girl with blue eyes before."

"Black *women* have many different eye colors. It's a genetic thing."

"I didn't mean no disrespect."

"Well, what I need from you is which apartment you are staying in, a phone number I can use to call you, and your whereabouts last night."

* * *

Hours later, Pro was typing up her report on the day's incidents. The manager at the apartment had been a pain but had become cooperative once she suggested she was looking at him as a suspect in May Johnson's death.

She wasn't, of course, because it all seemed to be a drug overdose. But, this way the manager would be careful not to go into the apartment for fear of leaving fingerprints.

She was looking forward to a date that night with her boyfriend of six months, Luther Ardoin. It would have to be an early night, because although May Johnson seemed straightforward, the other case, the knife slaying of Thomas James, would need a lot of follow-up work over the next few days.

However, in the back of her mind, something was off about the Johnson case. A drug overdose was common enough these days, but something didn't seem quite right.

Going through May's purse, she found things that didn't add up. First of all, there were no pills there. If May was an addict, she would be sure to carry a supply of the pain pills, even if they were hidden. Secondly, she was carrying pepper spray, and a small electric stun gun that shot electrodes into an assailant, even from fifteen feet away.

On one hand, these might be part of a single woman's arsenal, but it was unlikely that she would carry both the gun and the spray. Or maybe she was overly cautious.

Or maybe she'd been mugged.

Once Pro finished the report, she pulled up the files to see if May was listed on any police reports as the victim of a crime. She didn't find anything and it puzzled her. Why was May so careful?

"And hello to you," a voice said from the other side of her desk.

Pro looked up, expecting to see her partner, but behind Tom's desk and lounging in his chair sat her father.

"Max!" Pro snapped, annoyed that her sire had snuck into the bullpen and sat without her even noticing.

"Hey, pumpkin," Max said jovially. He was a tall man with a small beard and mustache, commonly called a "Van Dyke." His hair was white and he looked at her with eyes the same color as her own.

"Don't call me that," she hissed. "And get out of my partner's chair!"

Max rose with ease for a man in his sixties. He moved with the grace of someone who'd spent his life performing on stage. As he rose, a large silver coin appeared at his fingertips and was rolled down the knuckles of his long fingers.

"So, your mom and I haven't heard from you lately. Elisha is getting concerned she did something to make you mad."

Pro looked around to make sure they were the only ones currently in the bullpen. "Yes, she did. She started sleeping with you."

Max Martin, aka Max Marvell, the king of the Las Vegas magicians, frowned. "You know, some children of divorce would be thrilled that her parents were dating."

"Yeah, well, the last thing I want is to walk in on the two of you again," Pro bickered.

"The only time you 'walked in' on us was while we were sleeping."

"That was bad enough." Pro shook her head as if to remove the image. "What do you want, Max? I *am* at work."

"I wanted to ask you to come visit. Your mother and I want to talk to you about some things."

"You know the kind of hours I work, Max," Pro said and glared at her father. "And besides, I'm dating these days—"

"Which your mother and I are thrilled about. Luther is a good man."

"You only say that because every time he sees you, he wants you to do another magic trick."

Max lifted his chin haughtily. "Can I help it if your boyfriend recognizes talent when he sees it?"

Pro shook her head in disgust. Her father's antics tickled Luther, but Pro only found them annoying. "I'll see if I can get by this weekend."

"You could bring Luther," Max suggested.

Pro crossed her arms in defiance. "I'm working, Max."

"Yes, I saw on your computer. A woman found alone in a locked apartment. Might be right up my alley."

"It was probably a drug overdose, nothing more," Pro said and rose from her chair to block her monitor from her father. "And the last thing I need is for you to get involved in one of my cases."

"Come on, Pro. I helped with that one last month...."

"I wouldn't have even brought you in, and it was Tom that called you, not me."

"But I helped you two figure it out, right?"

Her lips formed a tight line. She had to admit, Max had pointed her and Tom in a direction that neither of them would have considered. But she'd be damned if she'd give him the satisfaction.

"Look, Max, I'm still sore at the stunts you pulled six months ago when you got into town. Breaking out of a cell and going behind my back—"

"But I helped on that case as well, pumpkin."

"Don't call me that," Pro snapped through clenched teeth.

"Oh well," Max responded airily. "Please call your mother."

"Will you stay away from the precinct if I do?"

"I'll do my best," Max said as he walked away.

Did he enjoy making her angry? It was the only explanation she could come up with.

She returned to her seat and typed away at the final line of her report. As she thought about it, she realized Max had been right. Pro had been avoiding her mother since she and Max began dating. A part of her felt like it was a betrayal.

Max had left New York, as well as his wife and child, when she was five with the offer of a stage show in a large casino in Las Vegas. At the time, Pro didn't know that Max wanted Elisha to move with him, and she had been too afraid that the show would fail and they would be broke. So Elisha stayed in NYC and filed for divorce.

Pro ended up being shuttled to Vegas for visits. But the redneck airhead named Trixie that Max had hooked up with made each visit unbearable. Elisha met and eventually married Joe Thompson, a beat cop who Pro considered her real father. Joe had passed away just two-and-a-half years ago, and for her mother to be sleeping with Max seemed an affront to his memory.

But, the few times she'd seen her mother, the older woman looked happier than she had in years. Joe's cancer and his death had worn her out emotionally and physically. To have the handsome, dashing Max Marvell come into town and pursue her had revitalized the fifty-something woman, and she seemed to glow with pleasure the few times Pro had seen her.

Add to that, Pro had to devote her free time to the relationship with Luther. She had to admit, now that she was getting sex on a steady basis, she had perked up a bit herself.

They had both been enjoying the relationship, though Luther's work in security and her work as a detective made getting together difficult. Sometimes, they met late after work and just went to her place or his and slept.

She filed her report, to be reviewed by Tom. She had to get out of there and enjoy one of her few early evenings with Luther. They were going to go out to dinner, like real people.

And *that* was a rare treat.

* * *

"Well, that was a nice dinner," Luther admitted as he took a sip from the glass of wine. They both only had one, as either of them could be called in at any moment—Pro because there might be a homicide and Luther because he was the site supervisor of a fancy condominium in Midtown.

They were in an outdoor cafe on Broadway just across from Lincoln Center. People in fancy clothes were going to the opera as the cool evening air blew down the avenue.

"Do you think we'll get through the night without anyone calling us?" Pro smiled.

"It has been known to happen. I've missed you, girl."

She leaned forward and rubbed his powerful arm. "I've missed you, 'fellow.'"

Luther laughed, his white teeth in contrast to his dark skin. He was a big man and well-muscled, with a shaved head and an upbeat personality.

"Okay, I deserved that," Luther chuckled. "You don't like to be called a 'girl.' I'll keep it to 'lady' or 'woman.'"

"Or 'goddess' might work." Pro smirked.

He leaned in. "Or 'temptress?'"

"Mm. I like the sound of that. Are you tempted?"

"Anytime I'm near you, Pro," Luther said.

They both leaned forward and kissed as the waiter slid the leather holder with the bill onto the table. Luther pulled back and grabbed the billfold.

"Let me chip in," Pro said and grabbed the large leather bag she carried.

"It's okay, Pro. I make more than you do, and I get my apartment for free," Luther said, as he slipped a plastic card in the leather wallet and held it up for the waiter to take.

"That seems so unfair," Pro replied, "with all the hours I put in."

The waiter took the binder and headed off to process the card. "Look, Pro, you wanna leave the NYPD and go into private security, you could make a bundle."

"Nah, I'm a cop. It's what I love," she responded. "But, I always wondered, you're in good shape. I am sure you could do a lot more than security on a condo."

Luther smiled. "I've done some of that in the past —bodyguard, armed security, even undercover—but I like to be in Manhattan. That way I'm available to be your plaything."

Pro narrowed her eyes. "And I intend to play quite actively tonight."

Luther smiled. "I could get into that."

The waiter brought the binder with the bill for Luther. The big man signed it, put his credit card away, and both he and Pro rose.

"My place?"

"I thought you'd never ask," she responded and indicated her bag. "I brought a change of clothes."

"Should I get you out of the clothes you're in, so they don't wrinkle?"

"I'm sure we can arrange something like that," Pro said as they stepped away from the restaurant and headed downtown.

"We could get a cab," Luther suggested.

"Let's walk. It's only ten blocks or so, and I want to work off the meal a little," Pro said and added with a wicked smile, "then I want my dessert."

They crossed the street and stopped to look at the huge open plaza in Lincoln Center. The buildings were lit to show the beautiful glass and marble construction, and they appeared like magical castles from the street. People in tuxedos and fabulous gowns were strolling about on their way to the ballet, opera, or some highbrow thing Pro had no interest in.

However, a small group had formed a circle around someone and she could hear a person talking loudly, or being amplified.

"Hey, it's a magician," Luther announced excitedly and began to move toward the crowd.

Luther loved magic, and Pro sighed in exasperation as she followed him toward the crowd. Why was it that any man in her life was a fan of magic? Her father, Luther, even the guy she used to date...

As they drew close to the crowd, the performer's voice grew clearer, more pronounced...and familiar.

An unreasoning fear hit Pro as her mind tried to grapple with what her senses were telling her. She began to whisper, "No...no...it can't be."

They reached the crowd and in the center stood a tall, good-looking man. He had reddish hair, a tight beard, and spoke with an Irish accent.

Pro stood next to Luther and leaned against him as her knees became weak. She was annoyed that this affected her so strongly. After all, she was a homicide cop; she could see bloodied corpses and take down suspects without working up a sweat.

But now she felt weak, lost, and was not comfortable with the feelings.

The man in the center of the crowd was Jamie Tobin, the Irish street magician Pro had had a torrid love affair with a year-and-a-half earlier. Jamie had lived with her for a month, but finally had to return to Ireland because his visa had expired.

Questions flooded Pro's mind: What was he doing here? Why didn't he at least call her? The last thing he'd said to her when they had parted was that he loved her. And now she was overwhelmed by the memory of the days and nights they'd spent together.

With a flourish, Jamie finished his routine, and the crowd around him clapped in approval.

"If ye enjoyed the show, give what ye can," he declared in a loud voice, and placed a can on the ground for anyone who wanted to make a donation. People began to put dollars into the container, and Jamie looked at the crowd.

His eyes met Pro's.

For a moment, she stood there and shivered, feeling naked before the stare of the man who had been her lover and had brought her to places no other man had been able to. Luther was a good lover, but Jamie had skills with his hands and mouth that had made her cry out over and over.

The fire she saw in Jamie's eyes made her want to run up and throw herself into his arms, but she was standing next to Luther, her big, strong boyfriend, and she grabbed his hand as logic flooded back into her brain.

She and Luther got along wonderfully, and he was a good man. Maybe not as exciting as Jamie, but he was solid and wouldn't be running off on her, like Jamie had done.

The momentary ache passed and she threw her shoulders back as the cop persona took over.

Jamie picked up the container and moved toward Pro and Luther.

"Hey, man, that was some good stuff," Luther said.

To Pro, it sounded like her boyfriend was a million miles away. She couldn't recall what trick Jamie had done, so surprised to see him that the performance had made no impression on her at all.

Jamie's eyes still burned into her, and she could feel herself weaken, but she bit her lip and stood even straighter.

Jamie glanced at Luther. "That's kind o' you, sir." His eyes moved back to her. "Why, Detective Thompson, it's been a while."

Pro fought to speak and worked to keep her voice calm. "Yes, it has. How have you been?"

Jamie smiled. "Well, I had that family issue in Ireland and just got back."

Luther frowned. "You two know each other?"

Jamie turned his gaze to Luther. "A passing acquaintance. We met on a case she was working on." His eyes returned to Pro and he smiled. "Back when she was a uniformed officer."

Pro felt herself blush. What was it about Jamie that could make her feel like a school girl?

Luther was looking at Pro and Jamie with suspicion. He was totally unused to seeing his girlfriend become tongue-tied around anyone, especially not some red-headed street hustler.

"Well, it was good to see you," Pro stated with as little emotion as she could.

"Please tell your mother I send me best," Jamie said.

Pro stared at the ground and gave a quick nod. "I will."

She grabbed Luther's arm and pulled him away, still flushed. She could almost feel Jamie's stare on the back of her head.

Luther walked with her in silence, as Pro forced her quickened breathing to slow and tried to regain control. Were there tears in her eyes?

She hated the idea that she could be thrown so easily by an old boyfriend. She had run into a former lover from the police academy, Julius Trent, numerous times and neither of them thought anything of it.

"So who was that guy?" Luther pestered. "And how does he know your mom?"

"He helped with a case. A magician had died, and he advised us."

"Like your dad?"

Pro stopped walking and glared at Luther. "No, not like my dad. He didn't push himself into the case; he just helped."

Luther held up his hands defensively. "Okay, okay, you don't have to bite my head off."

She stood there and tried to understand the mix of emotions she was going through. She had wanted to go with Luther and make love to him. But now, it was the last thing she could think of.

She looked at the ground, ashamed of herself, angry at her weakness. "Look, I have a crazy day tomorrow. I think I should go home."

Luther watched her, and she could almost feel his disappointment, like an energy pouring out of him. "If that's what you want, Pro."

She gave a curt nod and headed off to the subway that would take her to her apartment in Brooklyn.

As she walked, she allowed the tears to come.

2. Bill In Lemon

It took the subway ride to Brooklyn to get herself calmed down and thinking straight again.

And now she was angry.

How dare Jamie just show up like that and ruin her night? It was just like her father, showing up where she didn't expect and then making things all confusing.

Magicians were the worst.

Once over her initial shock, a part of her wanted to turn around and go back to Luther's. She would give him a lovemaking session that would make his head spin. She'd show that stupid Jamie that she had moved on with her life and was perfectly content with her new man.

She walked up the stairs out of the subway and onto the Brooklyn street to make her way to the small apartment. She lived in what could laughingly be called a "studio" or "efficiency" apartment. One main room with a tiny kitchen and a bathroom with a shower stall. It also had a walk-in closet that was actually larger than the kitchen.

But it fit her needs. She had a sofa that became a bed, and she could use the washer and dryer in the building. And most of her days were spent at the precinct and on-call, so she didn't need much.

As she unlocked the front door and walked up the flights of stairs, she decided she would have to make up the evening to Luther.

As she reached the top stair, she glanced up, and there stood Jamie leaning nonchalantly against her door.

At first, Pro was shocked and fought to catch her breath and found that her hand, on instinct, had located her service weapon in the large bag she carried.

She released the handgun and stared at her old beau.

"You got a lot of nerve showing up here."

He looked at her with a smirk. "You always did say I had a lot of nerve."

He spoke with that amazing Irish accent. Why did that always make her want him so badly? She had planned a night of lovemaking, and her body ached to be touched.

"You should leave before someone calls a cop," Pro chided as she took out her keys.

"I had to see you. I had to explain."

"Explain? Explain?" she snapped. "You go away, I get a couple of emails for months, and then you don't communicate, you don't even send a text in over a year."

A door opened on the floor below them and a voice shouted up, "Keep it down. Folks are tryin' to sleep."

Pro glanced at her watch. It was only 10:00 PM, but she had gotten rather loud.

"Please, Pro," Jamie whispered.

With an annoyed exhale of breath, she stormed to the door and unlocked the three locks, then held the door closed as she looked at Jamie. "You try anything and I'll break your arm."

"I have no doubt."

She flung the door open and Jamie stepped into the room. Pro was glad that she had taken the time to put the bed away and neaten up the room before she'd gone to work. Having to sit on the bed as they talked might be an open invitation for physical intimacy.

Jamie moved to the sofa and sat, as Pro took the padded chair near the window so there was distance between them.

"You want to explain?" Pro demanded. "Go ahead."

"I couldn't really reach out to ye," Jamie began, "because I was travelin'."

"Yeah, and there are no computers or phones where you were."

"Actually, I street-performed in piazzas in Italy, got hired for a show in Abu Dhabi. But I found a sponsor who paid my way back here to America."

She folded her arms. "A sponsor? And yet here you are, performing on the street."

"They cover me flight and apartment, but a little extra doesn't hurt, and the streets are the easiest way. Look, I only found out my visa had been approved to return to America two days before I had to leave."

"And how long do you get to stay this time?"

"Six months."

Her jaw was set. "So if I let you into my life, six months from now you'd leave me alone and heartbroken again."

He moved to one knee and slid across the wooden floor closer to her as he gazed up into her eyes. She kept her arms folded and leaned back from him.

"Believe me, Pro, I never wanted to hurt ye."

"Well, you did," she said, her jaw set. "You moved on and I moved on. I have a boyfriend and I'm fine."

"He seemed nice."

"He's not going anywhere." She stood, wanting to create space between them. Gazing into his clear green eyes only weakened her resolve. She moved to the door. "I think you need to go."

He rose. "The point is, I thought I moved on. I thought we'd both be better off if I didn't bother you. But when I saw ye tonight..."

She set her jaw, stared at the floor, and repeated in her mind, *I will not cry, I will not cry...*

He drew near. "Are you going to tell me you didn't feel it, too?"

She wouldn't raise her head. "I felt it as well," she admitted.

He put one finger under her chin and lifted it, as he brought his lips to hers.

Fire exploded through her as she was instantly and totally aroused. Every nerve ending screamed that she had to have this man—here, now, on the floor if necessary.

Through a force of will she ignored the unbidden desires and shoved Jamie back using both hands.

She was breathing hard, and every inch of her body was sensitive as if the slightest caress would push her over the edge.

"No," she stated half-heartedly. "I'm seeing Luther."

Jamie gaped at her. He had the appearance of a man who'd been struck in the head with a shovel, and Pro wondered if she wore the same expression of slack-jawed desire.

"I've missed you, Pro," was all Jamie could manage.

She had missed him as well—his clever hands, his sparkling wit, and the nights of passion that inflamed her.

But she knew magicians always leave.

"You need to go," Pro implored, her eyes on the floor. She couldn't fight it much longer, and if she met his eyes, she was lost.

"All right, *Storeen,*" he said, using the Gaelic word for "little treasure."

"Don't call me that," Pro insisted, still unable to look at him.

He reached into his pocket, pulled out a small note, and placed it into her hand. "Here is me phone number, if ye want to talk."

A part of her wanted to toss the paper into a nearby wastebasket, throw him out into the hall, and slam the door in his face. Another part of her, the one that was winning, wanted to rip his clothes off and become one with him.

He kissed her cheek, opened the door, and went into the hall and made his way to the stairs.

She moved to the door and wanted to fling it open and scream, "Come back!" Instead, she put the locks in place and made her way unsteadily to the nearby chair.

She was shivering with desire. On one hand, she thought she deserved congratulations for resisting his charms, and on the other hand, she cursed the fact that she was so overstimulated that she wanted to howl at the moon.

How dare he show up here and incite all these different feelings? She wanted to be angry and curse him for being born, yet at the same time she ached to make love and push her body against his, seeking fulfillment.

Instead, she went to the refrigerator, pulled out the large bottle of Chardonnay from the door, and poured herself a jelly jar full of the pale liquid.

She sat on the sofa and noted that she could smell his cologne, which caused another wave of desire to pass through her. She took a large sip of wine and noted that she still clutched the slip of paper tightly in her hand. After a few minutes and several sips, she calmed down. She took the paper and input the number into her phone so she would know it was him if he called.

That wasn't cheating.
Was it?

* * *

The next day she walked into the precinct and headed for her desk. She was grateful it wasn't as early as the previous day, as she'd awakened with a headache from the wine and the unsatisfied ardor.

This was the last thing she needed right now. Her busy work schedule could barely accommodate dating one man. There was no way she could date two.

She paused. *My God, am I seriously considering dating Jamie?*

She focused on moving to her desk and took another swig of her coffee. Of course she wasn't! She and Luther were getting along so well, and the long-term possibilities with the tall African-American man looked very good.

But had she ever desired Luther the way she had all but melted for Jamie last night?

She put it out of her mind, vowing to call her mother later. Maybe Elisha Thompson could give her some much-needed insight.

"Rough night?" her partner said from his desk as she sat.

She peered at him, bleary-eyed. "That's putting it mildly."

"Problems with Luther?"

"No, we went out to a really nice dinner last night, and then we walked through Lincoln Center and there was a magician—"

"Was it your dad?"

"Worse. It was Jamie."

Chu thought about this for a minute. "The redheaded guy? Didn't you use to date him?"

Pro leaned back in her chair. "As a matter of fact, yes."

Tom considered this for a moment. "Did he make a scene?"

She shook her head. "He didn't have to. Seeing him made me *very* confused."

"What are you going to do?"

"I have no idea," Pro said. "But now, I'm not sure what I want anymore."

"Don't let your memories be the deciding factor. We always remember relationships better than they actually were."

Pro nodded. "That's true. But I don't think I should take dating advice from you."

Chu held up his hands questioningly. "What do you mean? I've been dating one woman on a steady basis."

"And you won't introduce her to your parents."

He returned his eyes to the computer screen. "I thought we were talking about your problems, not mine."

Pro shook her head. "Does every man just avoid personal discussions?"

"Only the smart ones. Also the ME sent you the autopsy on May Johnson. Maybe we can clear that up today."

"That was fast." Pro pulled the report up on her screen.

"Seemed like a straightforward case, I guess."

Pro began to look over the report. "Did you read this?"

"Not really. I've been going over names of possible witnesses for the knife murder. The vic was Thomas James, and uniforms have been canvassing the neighborhood, collecting the names of anybody who may have seen or heard anything."

"Well, it looks like May Johnson isn't a simple case."

Chu glanced over. "Why, what is it?"

"The ME says she died from a broken neck. But the preliminary tox screen suggests that she had no opiates in her urine, and there were no pills in her digestive tract."

"So the ME is listing it as a homicide?"

"It would appear so," Pro said, going over the information a second time.

Chu rose and came around the desks that faced each other and stood behind Pro to look at her screen. "This is only the preliminary. I mean, a full toxicology report is going to take a couple days."

"I know," Pro agreed, "but I think we need to pursue this as a homicide."

Chu exhaled heavily. "Pro, I'm up to my eyeballs on the knife slaying. I have to interview witnesses the uniforms found. I really need to split that with you. I have about ten people."

"Okay, but I want to take some time to revisit the Johnson place this afternoon. That open window might have something to do with it, even though there were bars on it. I want to check that."

Chu put his hand on the desk as he leaned forward, his eyes still on the report. "Well, I could suggest someone who knows locks."

Pro glared at her partner. "Who?"

"A Vegas magician, who has been known to help the NYPD—"

"No!" Pro snapped, and then immediately lowered her voice. "You are not asking for help from my father!"

"Come on, Pro. We got these two cases, so we're stretched thin. And if anyone knows locks, it's your dad. He can open any lock that exists."

"Yes, but if we ask him to help then he'll think it's *his* case. He'll bother me day and night."

"How about if I ask him?" Chu suggested. "Have him meet us at the scene, keep it simple."

"Freakin' magicians," Pro fumed. "They do nothing but cause trouble."

She glared up at her partner who moved back to his seat and sat. She was angry, but she had to admit Tom was right. No one knew locks better than Max, and what's more, if there was a hidden way into May Johnson's apartment, her father would be able to find it.

"Okay," she finally relented. "But you call him, and tell him to just look at the scene and tell us what he sees, nothing more."

Chu smiled and pulled out his cell phone to call Max.

"Could today get any worse?" Pro muttered as Chu talked to her father.

3. Card Through Window

The interviews of neighbors at the brownstone where Thomas James had been killed took a few hours in the afternoon. Only a couple of residents were at home. Any other interviews would have to take place when people returned to their apartments after work, so Chu and Pro walked the two blocks to May Johnson's apartment at about 4:00 PM.

Pro's mood had not improved. The people they'd spoken to claimed little knowledge of Thomas James. The woman who lived in the apartment next to his claimed to have heard the noises that could have been an argument and a struggle at about 1:00 AM the night of the murder. But she had no idea who could have gotten into Mr. James' apartment or how, unless James had let them in.

All of this gave few clues, but she was sure both she and Chu would have to return to James' apartment now that forensics was done. They had decided to do so after they were done with Max's assessment of May Johnson's place.

Adding to Pro's confusion and annoyance, she got a text from Luther asking how her day was going. She texted him the first thing that came to mind: that she was busy and would get back to him later.

This had caused Pro to feel guilty, as she was basically blowing him off. But what could she tell him? Her mind envisioned some of the possible texts she could send: *That magician you met last night showed up at my apartment, and I almost slept with him.* That would not go over well. How about: *I think I want to date that magician you met last night, as well as you. How do you feel about being in a harem?*

She dismissed the idea of sending either text. She needed to focus on her job, which was pursuing two murders. Yet, thoughts of Jamie and Luther kept invading her mind. Murder cases were easy; relationships were just too complicated.

They arrived at the address for the Johnson apartment just as Max strolled up the street.

"Detective Chu, lovely to see you again," Max said and offered his hand for Tom to shake. "And Detective...Thompson...is it?"

"You're a riot, Max," Pro responded with her arms crossed.

"Good to see you, pumpkin." Max smirked.

Pro wanted to tell him not to call her that, but she bit her lip. His insights would be a help, though she didn't like it one bit.

"Hey, Max," Tom began, "we have a possible murder in a locked room."

"So you said on the phone. Show me the place. I don't know if I'll find anything, but I'll do my best."

"No gigs for wealthy clients?" Pro jibed.

Max smiled. "I always have time for you, Pro."

Pro nodded. "We are going into the apartment. It looks like the resident was murdered, but the scene was set up to look like a drug overdose."

"Someone staged the scene, eh?" Max said.

Pro headed toward the entrance, and Max and Chu followed, all three of them putting on latex gloves as they went.

"It could have been the neighbor with the spare key," Chu suggested.

"We could bring her in for questioning down at the precinct," Pro considered. "And that manager. He had to have a key."

Max spoke, "You mentioned there was an open window?"

"Yes, but with bars on it," Pro told him. "You want to take a look?"

"Always best to see the interior first," Max claimed with the air of an expert.

They walked down the hall and Pro turned to a doorway with yellow police tape on it that bore the warning: *Crime Scene Do Not Cross*.

Pro pushed the door open and they stepped into the apartment. Max immediately studied the room, looking up at the ceiling, but moved to the wall to put his ear to it and knock gently.

"We found the body in—" Pro offered.

"Not yet, please," Max intoned. He bent at the waist, and despite being as tall as he was, he peered under the chairs and sofa in the small living room.

Chu watched Max and looked to Pro questioningly. She appeared exasperated and shrugged at her partner.

All at once, Max stood up straight and glanced around the room one more time. "Okay, show me where the body was found."

Pro worked to keep her temper in check. She stepped to the door for the bedroom and opened it. "Right here, Max."

Max nodded and stepped quickly to the open door. Instead of going in, he stood and examined the room.

"The body was found—" Pro commenced.

"Right there," Max said as he pointed to the floor. "In the spot next to the bed and the bookcase."

Chu stepped behind Max. "Yes, how did you know?"

Max grinned as he looked back at the shorter detective. "It's the only place a body would fit."

Pro, tiring of the game, indicated the bathroom connected to the bedroom. "The open window was in here."

Max walked past Pro and quickly looked around the small bathroom. He went to the window, undid the latch, and easily lifted it.

"Fairly new window," Max noted. "It's vinyl, and double-paned glass."

"So what?" Pro snickered.

"Do you think it was replaced recently?" Tom put in.

Max studied the window frame. "There isn't a lot of dust, so it could have been a new install."

"That changes things," Chu said.

Although Pro resented her father being there, the detective part of her brain latched onto this revelation. "You think it was replaced for a reason?"

Max didn't look away from the window. "It's a possibility."

He reached out the open window and felt the bars, running his hand up and down as far as he could reach. "Fresh coat of paint on the bars, no rust to speak of."

He grabbed the large lock and rattled it in the hasp, then bent to peer at the lock. He stood up straight and turned to Pro. "I need to see the outside."

He stepped back from the window and moved quickly out of the bathroom, on his way to the apartment door.

"Do you mind staying here?" Pro asked Tom.

"No problem," Tom replied. "Go after him."

Pro nodded and took off after her father, using her long legs to catch up with Max's fast pace.

Her father headed out the front door of the apartment building and stepped into the narrow alley next to the building, heading to the back.

"Hold on, Max!" Pro called after him.

Max paused to turn back to his daughter and smile. "I think I know how the killer got in."

"That will help. You want to show me?"

The pair of them walked down the alley, passing apartment windows. Pro noted that the other windows on the first floor looked older. Those were wooden frames with paint beginning to peel and the protective bars showed spots of rust in several places. She reached out and grabbed one of the bars of welded metal and noted that the frame was solidly in place.

They continued heading toward the back of the building until they reached the window that was open. It was the one Max had raised in the dead woman's bathroom. Without any hesitation, Max stepped up to the window bars and gave them a pull.

Nothing happened.

Max stood back as Pro reached him. He bent and looked under the windowsill and at the top of the window where the metal frame was attached to the wall.

"Anything?" Pro badgered.

"Everything, to be honest," Max said. "These bars have been altered."

Pro frowned and walked up to the window to yank at the frame. It didn't budge. "Seems pretty solid, and there is that lock on the inside."

"To any casual burglar who might attempt to open it. But look on that edge." He pointed at the side of the frame that faced the street.

Pro looked at it carefully and noted a cylindrical tube of metal at the top and bottom. "The frame is on hinges. So what? We already knew it's supposed to open."

"Yes, all part of the design," Max confirmed. "What isn't part of the design is...this."

With the flair of a man who had been presenting miracles on stage for decades, Max touched the bottom of the frame and the entire metal contraption swung open.

Pro gasped in spite of herself and gazed at the open gate.

"You'll notice," Max pointed out, "that the lock is still solidly attached to the hasp, but the loop of metal, the shackle, is not connected to the wall. The shackle has been welded to the hasp."

Pro moved to the unhinged side of the frame and saw Max had been correct. The lock was still solidly in place, connected to the metal loop designed to secure it. But that loop had been welded to the long strip of metal that acted as the hasp.

Chu stood on the inside of the window and gazed out of the open space in amazement. "Pro, did forensics dust this thing for prints?"

"I doubt it," she responded. "We all thought it was an overdose."

Chu nodded. "I'll call them and get them back here."

"You might also want them to examine this," Max said and pointed in the corner of the windowsill. A small piece of black cloth was caught on the edge of a brick.

Chu leaned forward and looked at it. "I'll make sure they bag that."

"What is it?" Pro asked.

"Looks like fabric," Max surmised, "maybe from a coat or pants, when someone went through the window." He turned to face Pro. "You mentioned a superintendent. Is he in the building? Can we see him?"

Pro pulled her notebook and went through what she had recently written. "He has an apartment right on the first floor."

"Convenient," Max said and swung the bars back. The metal frame fastened into place with a *click*.

Pro looked at the window. "How does it open?"

Max put his hand on the corner where the frame met the sill. "There's a small catch right here. You have to know where it is to open it."

"If this was a murder, it was premeditated."

"So it would seem," Max agreed.

Pro led the way back into the building, texting Tom that she and Max were going to question the manager and gave him the apartment number.

Once in the hall, Pro knocked on the door and called out, "Mr. Schwartz? It's Detective Thompson. I have to ask you some questions."

The door cracked open only as far as the security chain would allow, and the unshaven man peeked out. "What?"

Pro put her badge into the space. "Mr. Schwartz, I need to ask you a couple of questions."

"Who's da guy?" Schwartz asked.

"Consultant. He's helping with the case."

The door closed and Pro and Max heard the chain slide off the door, then it opened wide to allow them access. Manny stepped back and Pro went in with Max behind her.

The apartment looked like it hadn't been updated in years. There was worn carpet on the floor and the furniture looked as if it had been purchased secondhand and then not treated well or cleaned for a long time.

Once again, Manny was in a flannel shirt, though this one was blue instead of red. The room was dark and the two small tables were caked with dust.

"Whaddya want now?" Manny complained. The little man had obviously gotten over his infatuation or intimidation around Pro.

Max jumped right in. "When was the window replaced in May Johnson's bathroom?"

Manny frowned. "Why do you gotta know that? And what's it got to do with the lady offin' herself?"

"We are now treating this as a homicide investigation, Mr. Schwartz," Pro informed him.

"Murder? Whaddya talkin' about? She got doped up and hit her head or somethin'."

Max cleared his throat. "Shall we focus on the matter at hand? We need to know when the window was replaced, and when the bars on the window were altered."

"What?" Manny asked.

"Just tell us when the window was replaced," Pro demanded.

"I dunno. I gotta look it up."

Max smiled. "Then I would recommend you do so, right now."

"Unless you want to do this at the precinct," Pro threatened, her hands now on her hips.

"Okay, okay," Manny said. "I got the receipts right here."

He went to a table and pulled open a large drawer, which contained a manila accordion-pleated folder.

He pulled out the oversized folder and sat in a large easy chair. The fabric was worn, and the padding underneath was beginning to show through. He started to go through the different pockets, each containing disorganized papers and invoices.

"The apartment is 1-E if that helps," Pro scolded.

"I know, I know," Manny whined.

He continued going through the large file, which apparently was not in any kind of order, until he pulled a yellow page out of one pocket. He held it out to Pro. "Dis is all I got."

Pro grabbed the paper and began to look it over. "The work was done a month ago? In the heat of August?"

"Yeah, the owner said something about the Johnson broad complainin' that the window was leaking after we had a bad rainstorm. She said her window was near a rain spout or somethin'."

Max and Pro exchanged a look.

"Pain in the ass if you ask me. There were these two guys I had to let into her place, and then I had to watch them."

"Did they work on the bars at all?" Max asked.

"Oh yeah, they had to get the rust offa 'em, do some welding and paint 'em," Manny explained.

Max turned to Pro. "Who was the contractor?"

"It's a place called Zelig Construction on 39th Street," Pro answered as she took out her phone and photographed the invoice.

"When can I get in dere?" Manny whined. "Look, the owner wants that place cleaned out and—"

Manny went on as Pro got a text and looked at her phone.

Max nodded sympathetically. "We'll let you know as soon as we can, Mr. Schwartz."

Pro looked up from her phone. "The NYPD will let you know as soon as we can release the apartment," she announced with a glare at Max. "We have to go. Tom has found something."

Without another word, Pro opened the door and headed out into the hall.

"Um...thanks for your help," Max attempted as he quickly followed. He caught up to Pro. "You were a bit rude with him, Pro."

Pro turned and faced her father, her eyes blazing. "Look, you do not tell people that 'We'll let you know,' Max. There is no 'we.' You are *not* part of this investigation."

"Okay, okay, I was trying to make the guy feel better."

"I would be concerned about that as well, if at our last meeting he didn't spend his time staring at my ass!" Pro told him and then stormed down the hall, moving faster than her father.

Max sighed and followed his daughter back into May Johnson's apartment.

"What's up?" Pro said as she walked in.

"I found something," Tom told her from the bedroom. Pro walked to it and Max followed but stayed in the doorway of the small room.

"Anything good?" Pro asked.

"I'm not sure, but it may change this entire case," Tom disclosed. He reached out and pulled one of the many books from the wall, a hardcover copy of a thick book entitled *In the Dark of the Night.*

"That she was a big reader?" Pro sneered.

Tom looked at her with a small smile. "Yes, but it was what she was reading."

He opened the cover and flipped past the first few pages. In the middle of the book, the pages had been cut away to form a large cavity.

"What was that for?" Pro asked as she reached out to touch where the book had been cut away. The pages with the open rectangle had been glued in place to form a solid protective wall.

"I would guess it was to hide something," Max suggested.

"I was confused as well," Tom acknowledged, "but it turns out that several of the books were prepared in the same way."

"So, she liked to hide things?" Pro wondered.

"Until I came upon this book," Tom said, and pulled down a book with a black and purple cover that was titled *The Muse.* Tom opened the pages, and the book also had an empty space in the middle of it. However, this one contained a large plastic bag filled with pills that to Pro's eye looked like OxyContin.

Pro reached out and touched the plastic bag, and then looked at the bookcases and the numerous books that adorned the shelves.

Pro nodded. "This changes things all right."

4. Book Of The Mind

The Crime Scene Unit arrived, and the team leader, Lieutenant Alex Jenkins, took Pro and Tom aside as his men went in.

He was a tall, heavyset African-American man with gray mixed into his dark hair. He showed up dressed in the coveralls the Unit members preferred. As his team began to photograph and catalogue everything in the apartment, the detectives brought him up to speed as Max waited down the hall.

"So how was all this missed?" Alex demanded, once they completed the explanation of the gimmicked window and the drugs in one of the books. The only books that had been doctored were titles Pro had never heard of, and all came from a publisher named "Brain Bender Press." On the spine of each of the prepared books was a small logo that showed an artist's concept of a brain.

Chu shrugged. "LT, this case appeared to be an OD. We only called in the Evidence Collection Team."

Pro nodded. "There was a murder scene a couple blocks from here, and the Crime Scene Unit was focused on that."

"So, this is now considered a homicide?" Jenkins asked.

"That was the ME's conclusion," Chu said. "Detective Thompson and I wanted to take another look before we called you in."

"We didn't know she had the supply of drugs," Pro added.

Jenkins glanced in where his three-person team was photographing the bedroom and opening books one at a time. "Well, if many of those books contained drugs, then your vic had to be selling."

"I would say she was a major dealer," another voice announced.

Jenkins looked up to see Max approaching. "Who are you?"

"He's our lock expert," Chu quickly offered.

Jenkins frowned. "You're the one who figured out that the bars on the window could open?"

Max nodded. "The victim may have been moving the drugs using that trick window. The manager said she was the person who demanded the window be replaced. Perhaps she made a deal with the contractor."

Jenkins focused on Max's face. "Hey, ain't you that guy from television?"

"I've been on a show or two," Max said modestly.

"Yeah, the magician from Vegas," Jenkins responded with delight. "Man, my wife and I caught your act! What a great show." He looked at the detectives. "This is your expert? How did you arrange that?"

"Detective Thompson is my daughter," Max explained with pride. "I help out when I can."

Jenkins looked to Pro, who reddened at the attention. Why did Max always have to embarrass her like this?

"Oh yeah, you two have the same eyes," Jenkins gushed. He turned to Max and gave his hand a hearty shake. "Well, nice meeting you. I'd better get in there and help my team."

"We should see if we can talk to the contractor," Chu said to Pro. "Did you get an address?"

"I photographed the invoice," Pro said, and pulled out her phone. "I'll text it to you."

"You said that the neighbor was the one that called in about May Johnson?" Max asked.

Chu had pulled out his phone to receive the image. "Um, yeah."

Max went on. "I think maybe you want to speak to her, if she is available. Perhaps she knew more about the drugs than she reported."

Chu and Pro exchanged a glance. Finally, Chu spoke, "We did only ask her about finding May."

"She's not at home, yet," Pro answered.

"Then we should talk to the contractor, and then come back here and speak to—what was her name again?"

"Tamela Irving," Pro said without hesitation.

"Let's head to the contractor's office and back up here later," Chu agreed, then turned to Max. "Thanks for your help, Max."

Max held up both of his hands. "Hold on. You haven't let me see the other crime scene."

Pro gritted her teeth. "That's a different case, Max. It has nothing to do with May Johnson."

"Really? How did the killer leave the scene?" Max asked.

Chu frowned. "We assume through the front door."

"Was there a blood trail?" Max insisted. "Was there evidence whoever it was went through the front door?"

Pro and Chu exchanged a glance. Finally, Tom spoke, "How do you know that?"

"I glanced over the report on Pro's desk when you called me in."

"That was confidential, Max," Pro fumed.

"I think these two cases are related," Max explained.

Chu's eyebrows went up. "Do you have any proof of that?"

Max gave a half-smile. "Let me take a look at the crime scene and I'll give you some."

Pro turned to her partner. "This is nuts. He has nothing."

Chu glared at Max but then turned to his partner. "I'll take him over for a look around. You hang here and see if the witness shows up or if Jenkins and his team find anything to advance our case."

Pro's mouth fell open. "You're letting him see the crime scene for Thomas James?"

"If it'll help, I'd let anyone with a good idea see that scene," Chu said, then turned to Max. "Okay, Mr. Marvell, let's go."

Pro hated it when Chu pulled rank and made her feel like the junior partner. Even though she was younger than him, and indeed *was* the junior partner. But most of the time she felt like they were equals.

But he didn't know that Max was just trying to force himself into the investigation. This was why she didn't want him involved. She had to admit that he found the trick window when they never would have, but even so!

She tried to calm herself, but then a text appeared on her phone that distracted her.

It was from Jamie.

It read: *I want to see you. I can't stop thinking about you. Tell me you hate me and I won't bother you, but if there is a chance you still feel something, let me know.*

Pro leaned with her back against the wall and stared at the message. She had blown off Luther's text, but this one made her heart hammer in her chest.

What should she do?

She quickly texted her mother: *Can I come by and talk to you tonight? Need advice. Confused.*

It only took a moment for Elisha to respond: *Glad to help, but your father will be here.*

She gave an annoyed groan, and then texted: *Need to talk in PRIVATE.*

Will figure something out, was the response.

That wasn't much help.

Now, what to do about Jamie? She wanted to text him: *You've got a lot of nerve,* or, *It would be best if you don't try to contact me.*

That was the correct response. That was the way you kept your life on its proper path. You didn't give in to crazy desires and spend time with men who weren't good for you.

Instead she typed: *Seeing my mom tonight. Maybe tomorrow?*

She hesitated for a moment, then sent the text.

"Damn, damn, damn," she whispered to herself.

"Everything all right, detective?" Jenkins said from the doorway, which made Pro jump.

"F-fine," she stammered. "Just an...um...annoying text. Old boyfriend."

This made Jenkins chuckle. "It takes a pretty special person to be with a cop. The stuff my wife has put up with for twenty years, you wouldn't believe: missed dinners, missed parties, missed birthdays... and I won't even mention holidays."

"I guess so," Pro responded.

Jenkins gave her a smile and went back into the apartment.

Pro had given a simple answer, but she knew. Her step-father, Joe, was a beat cop, and even though his hours were steadier than a detective's, he often had to run off to help in an emergency, or go in to work a case that needed him during school events and social engagements. The life of a cop was hectic and it took an unusual person to keep up with it.

That's why Luther Ardoin was such a logical choice. He worked in security; his father had been a cop. He was flexible and supportive, and he would stand by her and with her.

Jamie Tobin was a fly-by-night magician, who breezed into town and wooed her when it suited him. So why did his presence weigh on her heart? The thought of being with him again made her knees go weak. Memories of their lovemaking flashed through her mind and she could feel a warmth spread through her body.

She shook her head to snap out of it. She was on duty, and falling into a lustful fantasy, no matter how pleasant, was definitely not okay.

She was glad she was alone in the hall because she was sure her face was flushed and her breathing had quickened. Just as she calmed herself, a mature African-American woman came down the hall. She was average height with a round face and dreadlocks going down her back. She was dressed in a brightly colored jacket over a pantsuit and boots. Pro stepped out to greet her and made sure her shield was in plain sight on her belt. "Ms. Irving?"

The woman paused and looked at Pro. "You were one of the detectives from the other day, weren't you?"

"Yes, ma'am. We met only briefly, but I'd like to ask you a couple more questions if you have the time."

"I can't think of anything else I could offer," Tamela suggested as she moved to her apartment door across the hall and unlocked the two locks. "Poor May, dying all alone like that."

"That's the thing, Ms. Irving," Pro stated plainly. "We are now looking at this as a homicide."

She looked back at Pro with a combination of surprise and fear. "Oh my. Do I need to talk to a lawyer?"

Pro smiled. "Ms. Irving, you aren't a suspect. But perhaps you are aware of more than you think. I just want to ask you a few questions."

Tamela gave a suspicious glance to the open door to May Johnson's apartment and nodded. "Come on in, I guess."

The 1-F apartment was a little larger than the one across the hall, but not much. The living room was simple but neat as a pin. Tamela obviously cared about keeping the place nice.

"Can I get you some tea?" Tamela asked, and moved toward the small kitchen area.

"No, that's fine. So were you aware of any of Ms. Johnson's activities?"

"I knew she liked to go walking. Got me into it. And there was that book club she went to every Thursday night."

Pro's head snapped up. "Book club?"

"Yes, they met every week."

"What did that entail?" Pro asked, keeping her voice calm. She pulled out her notebook and pen.

"Oh? Let's see. They exchanged books, and from what May told me, they talked about them. They would meet at the Chelsea Piers."

"So she would take books with her every week?" Pro said and scribbled as she spoke.

"Yes, every week she'd return the book she was reading and she'd always come home with a new one."

After she added the drugs, or is that where she got them? Pro thought. "And you say she did this on Thursdays?"

"Yes, does that help?"

"It does, Ms. Irving. I need to speak to my associates for a moment," Pro told her and moved to the door. She stepped outside and into the opposite apartment. "Lieutenant!"

Jenkins moved to the door. "What is it, detective?"

"Please keep your eye out for anything like a calendar or a flyer about a book club."

Jenkins frowned. "You onto something?"

"Maybe. The vic went to a book club, and considering where the drugs were stashed—"

"It might be important. We'll look, detective, but if her calendar is on her phone or computer, you'll have to have the Cyber Unit go through it."

"Did the Evidence Collection Team find a smart phone?"

Jenkins frowned. "I don't have that report. That would go directly to you."

"Right, that's right," Pro grunted.

"But if we find one, I'll let you know." Jenkins smiled.

"Thanks, LT," Pro said with relief, just as the text alert went off on her phone. She pulled it out, and there was a message from Chu.

Please come to scene right away. Important.

* * *

It only took a few minutes for Pro to walk the two blocks to the apartment where Thomas James had been murdered. She let Lieutenant Jenkins know she was leaving. She also requested Ms. Irving if they could speak another time and made sure she had the woman's phone number.

Once she reached the other building, she found that Julie Barker was at the front door.

"Officer?" Pro asked. "Is there a problem?"

"I'm not sure, Pro," Julie said. "I got a call from Tom and he told me he needed an officer to watch the door here. I thought the scene had been released."

"So did we, Julie. Is Bailey around?"

"No. We were at a bust, and he had to stay."

Pro went down the hall and was struck again by the similarities of this building to the one where May Johnson was killed. A four-story brownstone, with the victim's living quarters on the first floor.

She reached the apartment and knocked on the door and was surprised that Max opened it.

"Pumpkin! You made it here fast." Max smirked.

"Don't call me that! Where's Tom?"

Still smiling, Max stepped inside. "He's in the bathroom, next to the bedroom."

"What was so important?"

"You have to see it," Max told her, still smiling.

Annoyed by Max's glee, Pro moved quickly to the bedroom. She hadn't really been in here the last time, as the body was in the living room. Bloodstains were still on the floor from the knife attack that had ended Thomas James' life.

As she went into the bedroom she noted that there were several bookcases in there as well. It was larger than May Johnson's, and the bookcases were freestanding, not built into the wall.

She turned the corner into the bathroom and found Tom standing next to an open window, holding a book. Through the window, Pro could see Max standing outside in the alley. How did he get there so fast?

He stood with the protective window bars, but they were opened out into the alley on the built-in hinge, and Pro could see the lock fastened to the hasp and not the wall, just like at the other apartment.

She gasped in surprise. "You have got to be shitting me!"

Tom shook his head. "Max found it in two minutes. Plus, the books? Many of them have got that space in the center as well." He opened the book and like the ones from May Johnson's, it was hollowed out. "And look, same publisher."

Chu closed the book and showed the spine. The little brain logo was on it with the words "Brain Bender Press" underneath.

Max leaned into the window. "Seems like our two murders are linked."

Pro sighed. "So it would appear."

5. Inexhaustible Bottle

Pro sat in the back of the taxi next to her father, fuming.

"Okay, I'll let you two talk without me," Max was saying. "Once I see your mother, I'll go out and get wine or something."

"I don't see why you are going up there at all."

"Well, your mother and I need to talk to you about some things."

Pro crossed her arms. "What things?"

Max faced forward. "She wants both of us to discuss it with you."

"Fine," she snapped. "Since when did you become such a wuss?"

"Since I decided I didn't want to anger your mother. You and she have the same temper."

"My temper is fine," she said calmly.

"Sure, pumpkin."

"Don't call me that," she barked.

They continued the journey in silence.

The cab pulled to the curb on West End Avenue in the 80s, letting Max and Pro out. The pair crossed the street to the building that towered fifteen stories overhead.

They were met by a doorman who smiled in recognition when he saw the pair of them. Max pulled out a key for the lobby and opened the door.

"You got a key now?" Pro huffed.

Max held the door for her. "It made things easier."

"Just like always," Pro said as they walked to the elevator. "Mom lets you get away with anything."

They were soon on their way to the correct floor. Max let Pro go first, and she pulled out her own key to open the door to the condominium. "I suppose you've got a key for this door as well," she muttered.

"It would make sense," Max attempted.

They walked in to find Elisha standing near the door. "There's my warrior," she said to Pro and opened her arms to give her a hug.

Max moved past them and into the living room.

"So, you gave Max a set of keys," Pro chided. "Not that he couldn't just pick the lock if he wanted to come in."

Elisha took a deep breath. "Yes, well, Pro, why don't you sit down?"

She gestured to the sofa, and Pro moved to it to sit. Her mother remained standing, and Max came over to take her hand.

Elisha glanced at Max and went on. "I've...we've... been meaning to talk to you about some things."

Max cleared his throat. "You see, your mother and I really have been enjoying spending time together."

Pro crossed her arms and leaned back. "I know. He's been here practically every time I've come by."

Max and Elisha exchanged guilty glances. Finally, Elisha said, "I know, honey. And that's because Max lives here now."

Pro jumped to her feet, her mouth agape. "What?"

Max went on hurriedly. "We decided months ago that me staying in hotels or trying to get a place just didn't make any sense."

"Months ago!" Pro seethed. "This happened months ago and you didn't tell me?"

"We didn't want to just spring it on you," Elisha said. "Besides, we wanted to make sure it would work."

"So you let Max just walk in here and take Joe's place, just like that?"

"Oh come on, Pro," Elisha said.

"What about Joe's stuff?"

Max lifted a finger. "We put what we didn't give away into storage with my equipment. I have a warehouse in New Jersey—"

"Just like that! Without even asking me?" Pro raged.

Elisha's hand went to her hip. "Since when do I have to ask you about *my* apartment? Or who I choose to sleep with?"

"You've lost your mind, Mother!"

"Why don't I go out and get some wine?" offered Max. He let go of Elisha's hand and headed for the door.

"Coward!" Pro yelled after him.

"You know it," Max said as the door shut behind him.

The two women glared at each other.

"It makes sense, honey," Elisha began, her voice quieter. "Getting a place in New York is expensive, and I have plenty of room—"

Pro glared at the floor. "And all of Joe's things are gone?"

"He don't need them anymore, Pro."

"It's not fair," Pro sulked. "Joe's dead, and Max just gets anything he wants."

"Well, in this case, I want Max as well."

Pro lifted her head, her eyes wet. "What do you mean?"

"I was lonely, honey."

"You had me."

"Once or twice a week, and I had friends. But I'm not all that old, honey. I wanted a man in my life, and Max is a much better man now that he isn't worried about fame and fortune anymore."

"I just hate the idea of you replacing Joe."

"I didn't replace Joe. Joe will always be a part of me, and we had many good years together. But, your father loves me."

"Loves himself, I think," Pro grumbled.

"And I've fallen in love with him, too, all over again."

Pro looked at her mother. Elisha had blossomed in the last half year. She'd been more upbeat and happy, and Pro grudgingly had to admit it was probably Max's influence.

"I guess...if you're happy," she finally mumbled.

Elisha came over to her daughter and took her into a hug.

"I got to admit, I like having sex again."

Pro pushed her mother away. "Mom! Ew!"

Elisha smirked. "For a young woman, you're a prude."

"As is anyone when they think about their parents having sex. Ew! So, how does Max amuse himself when you're at work?"

Elisha was a much sought after designer and still put in at least forty hours per week at her own business.

"I have to admit he's a bit bored. At first, he was busy having all his equipment moved to New Jersey and getting it all set up the way he wanted. But now that's done, and he wants to take me on trips."

"Is that what you want?"

"I still like working at my business, but I do plan to take *some* time off; just not as much as Max would like."

"Explains why he keeps visiting me at work."

Elisha sighed. "I just hope he finds something to fill his time a bit more. It's not like he needs the money." She moved to the armchair and sat. "But, how can I help you? You texted me that you needed to talk."

Pro moved back to the sofa.

"Are things all right with Luther?" Elisha worried.

"Yes. No, I mean, I'm confused."

"Why, honey?"

She met her mother's eyes. "Jamie is back in town."

"Jamie Tobin? The magician?"

Pro nodded. "I saw him street-performing...with Luther."

"That must have been awkward."

"It ruined my plans for the evening, and I guess Luther's as well. I didn't know that seeing him after all this time would hit me the way it did."

"I see."

"And then when I got home he was waiting at my apartment."

"Really?"

"He told me he still has feelings for me."

"And do you have feelings for him?"

Pro bit her lip. "I didn't think so. But then he kissed me."

"Ah."

"Mom, I almost…I mean…I wanted him…bad."

"How much?"

"Like pin him to the floor and have my way with him."

Elisha lifted an eyebrow. "That much, huh? Did you?"

"What?" Pro responded, shocked. "No, I'm dating Luther. I sent Jamie away."

"I see. But you wanted to make love with Jamie?"

Pro stared at the floor again. "With every fiber of my being. And now he's texting me, says he wants to see me, and I don't know what to do."

Elisha nodded. "Because if you see him again, you don't think you'll be able to resist."

Pro's cheeks flushed. "Luther is wonderful and sweet. But Jamie is the best lover I ever had."

Elisha paused to consider this. "I understand. It was the same way with Joe and your father."

"Joe was a better lover?"

This made Elisha chuckle. "No, Max wins in that category. He's a showman and always puts out the extra effort."

"Please don't tell me any more," Pro begged.

"The point is, what makes a real relationship isn't the chemistry between the sheets. It's the day-to-day things that make the difference."

Pro pondered this for a moment. "So how is it living with Max?"

"He can be demanding and selfish, but I call him out on it when he is. He truly is better than he used to be, and he's trying very hard to make me happy."

"Because he loves you."

Elisha smiled. "That's right. And after the multiple wives he's had, and the spotlight in Vegas with his own show, he doesn't have anything to prove anymore. He's a lot more relaxed than he's ever been, and he just enjoys life and makes me enjoy it along with him."

"That's nice," Pro conceded.

"It would be good if you found that out before you're as old and gray as your mother."

"You look great, Mom," Pro insisted. "And Max is lucky to have you."

"As I remind him every day," she chuckled.

There was the sound of the key in the door, and Max came into the room with a paper bag that held a bottle of wine. "Is it safe, or should I hide in the bedroom?"

"Just give us a couple more minutes, Max," Elisha told him.

"Okay," Max said and placed the bottle on the nearby table as he went into the bedroom and shut the door.

"So, what are you going to do?"

Pro paused. "I think the best solution is to meet Jamie someplace public and tell him not to bother me anymore."

"Uh-huh," Elisha agreed.

"I mean, he's only here for six months and then he's gone. I have to think long-term."

"Sounds very rational."

Pro sighed. "Now I just have to convince my heart of it."

"Or any other parts of your anatomy," Elisha joked.

"Why is it that when you recall a lost relationship, it always seemed so good? Especially the sex?"

Elisha gave a glance at the closed bedroom door. "And sometimes it's *better* than you remember," she said with a knowing wink.

"Ew, Mom."

* * *

Pro arrived back in Brooklyn and was greatly relieved when Jamie was not skulking around her small apartment.

As she undressed for bed, she quickly sent a text to Luther: *Sorry I was preoccupied today. The double murders appear to be linked. I'll need a few days.*

She sent it. A few days would give her a chance to get everything sorted out and give Jamie the heave-ho. She also sent the young magician a text: *Meet me tomorrow at 8:00 PM at the Magnolia Bakery, 69th & Columbus.*

She sent it, then put on a set of pajamas and pulled out her bed. She threw a blanket on top as the autumn night had grown chilly and got under the sheets.

Her phone made a tone as she received a message from Luther: *It's okay. Things are busy here. End of the week looks good.*

She smiled. Luther was always so considerate. He understood how committed she was to her career and gave her the space she needed.

The phone vibrated again, and a message appeared on the screen from Jamie: *I will be there. So want to see you.*

She sighed. It would be tough, but better to do it in person than just send him a text. She wanted to be friends with Jamie; she just didn't want to desire him anymore.

She put the phone on its charger and lay back in bed. She started to slip into a place between reality and sleep. She was drifting and found her mind went to the last time she and Jamie had made love—a year and a half ago on this very bed. He was leaving on a flight the next day, and it was their final opportunity to be intimate after a month of living together.

His strong fingers had touched her body so gently and made her quiver with desire as he caressed every part of her slowly, making her ache with longing. His lips touched her mouth, her breasts, and then lower until he was kissing her core, his lips and tongue driving her mad. Then he moved into her, inside of her, and she took him not only into her body, but into her heart.

Pro gasped and sat up in the bed, as an unexpected climax rushed over her. She had gripped the blanket tightly in both hands and moaned out loud as wave after wave pulsed through her.

She sat there and tried to catch her breath, then got up to go to her tiny bathroom and clean herself.

"Bastard," she muttered under her breath. "He doesn't even have to be here to make me do that."

However, she found when she got back in bed, she went off to sleep with a contented smile on her face.

6. Asrah Levitation

Very early the next day, while most New Yorkers slept, Pro worked out a good hour in the gym near her apartment. It wasn't much to look at and attracted only older boxers and brusque men, and carried a smell that combined old sweat with mold. But it had what Pro needed.

She went through her routine with the free weights, then used her leather gloves as she warmed up on the speed bag. After that, she went to town on the heavy bag. She made sure to practice all of her strikes, not just with her hands, but all of her kicks, as well as her elbow jabs. She was glad to do something to release her pent-up anger and energy, and she hoped it would help her sublimate the sexual longings that had troubled her the previous night.

She also wanted to make sure that her moves were instinctual. As a detective, there were not a lot of occasions where she took down a perp, but she was aware that her body must always be prepared to be able to do so. The idea of the fat, donut-eating cop was rare among the people who were out in the street every day.

She finished up, feeling relaxed, headed home, and hit the shower before she headed into Manhattan and her precinct.

When she arrived, Tom was going over the forensic reports, and Pro pulled up information on her computer screen so they could compare notes. Since their desks were pushed together, they faced each other, and as one finished a page, he or she would pass it to the other to review.

Tom spoke first, "So, the pills we found are made to look like OxyContin, but they were actually Fentanyl."

Pro nodded. "Yes, and loaded with impurities. The drugs in those books could have caused a lot of overdoses."

"Well, we got some of it off the street." Tom grimaced.

Pro nodded. "Afraid it wasn't much, considering how many hollowed-out books they both possessed. But that leads to the question: If both James and Johnson were killed for the drugs, how did *any* of the drugs get left behind?"

Tom sat back in his chair. "The killer could have been in a hurry and overlooked the one book we found. My question is: Did the killer know about the trick windows?"

"We have to assume he did," Pro said.

"So what's our next step?"

Pro considered this. "My first suggestion would be to track down May's book club."

"Why?" Chu pushed, but gave her a look that suggested he'd thought the same thing.

"The drugs were in books, she was part of a book club; it seems a logical place to start," Pro insisted. "Any luck with a phone for her, or anything with a calendar?"

Tom reached over and grabbed one of the sheets of paper off Pro's desk. "Not in her purse or in the apartment."

"But they found a monthly bill for a mobile phone in the apartment," Pro said as she noted a line on the report from the Crime Scene Unit. "We need to get a tracer on the phone, see if it's still active."

"Already done, Pro. I got the Cyber Unit on it first thing this morning."

Pro sighed. "I'm glad one of us is on the ball."

"You do seem a little distracted. Are you all right?"

Pro looked at her partner. They shared so much, and she even had insights from Julie Barker that Tom hadn't shared. She paused and then said, "You remember that I ran into Jamie, that street magician?"

"Yeah, sure. You said he showed up at your place and made you feel confused?"

"Not anymore. After work, I am going to meet with Jamie in a public place and tell him that Luther and I are serious."

"Why don't you just text him?"

Pro shook her head. "Guys are so cold."

"I don't know," Tom said. "It seems kinder. I mean, you meet with him and he sees what he's losing. That seems meaner to me."

"I hope you treat Julie better than that."

Tom looked around the bullpen, worried. "Keep that to yourself."

"Relax, no one knows who I'm talking about." Pro grinned but lowered her voice. "So, you gonna propose or what?"

Tom hung his head. "I'm meeting a Korean girl at my parents' tonight."

"What? A date?"

"Sh! I...guess you could call it that."

"That's crazy!"

"I know, I know, but what can I do?"

"Tell your parents to butt out and propose to Julie," Pro hissed.

"I can't, Pro. Korean parents are very involved in their children's lives."

"Well, un-involve them."

"Can we just talk about the case?" Tom fretted.

Pro leaned back. "As soon as my partner grows a pair."

"The case, Pro?"

"Fine, fine. We should talk to the contractor and see if we can track down who did the work on the bars."

"That's something I can get behind," Tom said, and stood, pulling his suit jacket off his chair and putting it on.

Pro closed the file on her computer, then grabbed the assorted papers on her desk, put them in a folder, and locked them in a drawer.

"Why are you locking it?" Tom mused. "We're in a police station."

"When my father met us here yesterday, he took a look at some of the reports."

Tom chuckled. "Your father is something."

They moved toward the stairs to exit the precinct.

"Now he thinks the double murders are 'our' case," Pro said as they walked down the steep stairs. "This is exactly what I was afraid of. This is why I don't like to bring him in on a case."

"I don't think we could have figured out how to open those metal bars without him," Chu pointed out. They walked to the nearby unmarked police car and got in.

"Yes, but now he feels he's entitled to be part of our investigation," Pro complained. "Honestly, if the man wants to be a cop he should just go to the academy."

"I didn't think they took retirees." Chu smirked as he pulled the car into traffic and headed downtown on Seventh Avenue.

"He could probably pass the physical part of the requirements."

"I'd love to see him sprint the fifty yards." Chu smiled. "I guess you're glad they limit entrance to thirty-five year olds."

"If they didn't, I wouldn't put it past him," Pro opined.

Chu pulled the car onto 39th Street and headed west, pulling over between Ninth and Tenth Avenues. The roar of buses from the nearby Port Authority Bus Terminal filled the air, and the pair of detectives crossed the street and went into the small doorway to the first floor of a nearby building.

Pro pushed the buzzer, and a makeshift curtain was pulled away from the glass at the door. On the other side of the window appeared a large man. He was grizzled, had a long mustache, was dressed all in denim, and looked like he could bench press a Buick. "Yeah, whaddya want?" he shouted through the glass.

Pro and Chu held up their shields, and the man's eyes grew wide and he pulled the door open. "Look, I don't know nothing about those two guys I hired to work on that fence. I thought they were legal—"

"We are looking for Mr. Zelig," Pro said.

"That's me," Zelig replied, looking Pro over as if she were the most amazing female he'd ever seen. "What are you, six feet tall?"

Chu moved forward to distract the big man. "We are just checking up on a job you did."

He looked confused by this. "Why, something wrong with it?"

Chu pulled up the crime scene photos on his phone and showed the view of the window with the bars in place behind it. He turned the photo to the man. "You replaced a window on an apartment on 52nd Street, a month ago. Apartment 1-E."

Pro pulled up the invoice on her phone and held it out as well. The man's eyes went from one smart phone to the other.

"Let me take a look," Zelig said, and went to his desk and to the computer. In mere moments, he was looking at his copy of the invoice. "Yeah, that was my guys. But I checked the job before we billed him. Everything looked copacetic to me."

Chu pulled up a photo with the window open and the bars open behind it. He then turned his phone to the seated Mr. Zelig.

Zelig studied the photo and said, "It's supposed to do that. In case there's a fire."

"Yes, but look where the lock is," Chu said and pinched the screen to expand the photo.

Zelig looked again. "Hey, is the lock closed?"

"Yes, it is," Chu explained.

He frowned. "It ain't supposed to do that."

Pro spoke up. "We also found a catch that allowed the bars to be opened from the outside."

Zelig's attention moved to Pro. "My guys did that?"

"We don't know, but we need to speak to them," Chu told him stone-faced.

"Sure, sure," Zelig said, and looked at the computer again. He pulled up a calendar and it listed several sites and who was assigned to each one. "Yeah, that was Tony Morales and Jesus Alvarez."

The big man pulled a sticky note and wrote down an address, as Pro wrote the names in her notebook. Zelig offered the note to Chu. "This is the site where they are today. I got a three-man team; they're doin' a sidewalk."

"They do metalwork one day and masonry on another?" Pro asked.

"Yeah, those two work all the time because they got skills. I mean, ironwork, carpentry, masonry. Those guys just got a talent for it, and they're hard workers. I can always count on 'em showing up."

"Anything else you can tell us?" Chu asked, eyeing the contractor.

Zelig paused and looked down. "They...might...have a record."

"A police record?" shot Pro.

Zelig spread his hands in an "I don't know" gesture. "I've heard...y'know...from some of my guys that they got gang tats and might've done time. But, I gotta tell you, I ain't never had no trouble with them."

Pro shook her head, unsure of Zelig's triple negative, and decided it was better to not push it.

"Thank you for your time, Mr. Zelig," Chu said as the detectives moved to the door.

Zelig stood and offered his card. "Well, if you take 'em in, you let me know."

"Nice that you care about your employees," Chu mentioned as he took the card.

"Nah, if they get arrested, I got jobs to cover."

Chu and Pro crossed the street and returned to the car.

"Where to?" Pro asked as they got in and Chu gunned the engine.

"353 West 56th Street," Chu replied as he handed the sticky note to Pro. "Look up the names, see if they *do* have a record."

Pro pulled up a laptop computer mounted on a hinged metal frame in the car so it could be pushed out of the way. She quickly input the names.

"I'm getting several hits on the name 'Tony Morales.' It would help if I had a description."

"Well, we will see them in a few minutes."

"I have only one Jesus Alvarez, and he has been involved in gang activity," Pro said. "I'm looking at his mug shot."

"So, one of them we will recognize," Chu exhaled.

"You think they're the ones that gimmicked the windows?" Pro asked.

"If they didn't, they probably know who did."

Moving east on 56th Street, Tom pulled the unmarked to the legal side to park the car.

They both came out of the vehicle where a man was working on a freshly poured square of concrete, using a wooden float to smooth out the surface.

The man looked up as the detectives approached. "Tony Morales or Jesus Alvarez?" Chu said while holding up his badge.

The man gestured over to a waist-high wall in front of a nearby building. There stood two men, their skin a dark tan, and in the middle of them was Max doing a card trick as the two men laughed and hooted.

Pro moved quickly to the three men. "Max, what are you doing here?"

The two men looked apprehensive at the approach of the tall woman with the badge on her belt.

"Relax, Pro," Max said, and turned to the men, putting up his hands in a calming manner. "*Esta mujer es mi hija.*"

The two men visibly relaxed.

"What're you saying?" Pro demanded.

"I just told them you're my daughter," Max disclosed.

One of them looked Pro up and down and said, *"Ella es hermosa."*

"No tan hermosa, como su madre," Max told them, which made both men chuckle. He looked at Pro and explained, "He said you were beautiful, and I said they should see your mother."

"Max, we need to question these men," Chu said.

"No need, I already did. I have their contact information, and they are both willing to come to the precinct to give a statement if you need them," Max said with a smile.

"Max, one of them might have a criminal record," Pro hissed at her father.

"No, they both do. But they are trying to change their lives." Max turned to the men again. *"Estás cambiando tu vida?"*

Both men nodded and said, *"Si, si."*

"This doesn't help us, Max," Chu said.

"Sure it does. Morales told me that welding the lock and putting in that catch was on the plans he was given for the job."

"What, from Zelig?"

"Zelig told them the plans would be there, but here is the weird thing. They came in the first day and only had time to replace the window. When they got there the second day, the plans were different."

"Someone switched them?" Pro gasped.

The taller of the two men, Alvarez, who Pro recognized from his mug shot, spoke up with a heavy accent. *"Si,* plans, they different."

Chu replied, *"Tu jefe los cambió?"*

Pro stared at her partner in disbelief. Did everyone speak Spanish except her?

"No lo sé," admitted Morales.

"Your partner asked if the boss changed the plans, and Mr. Morales doesn't know," Max translated. "But he did what the plans told him."

"How did they do such a sophisticated hidden catch?" Pro asked.

Max stepped in. "They told me it was in the plans, and that the hardware was resting on top of them. The same thing the next day when they fixed the bars at James' apartment."

"They did both jobs!" Chu exclaimed.

"Yes, though they didn't know that it was Thomas James' apartment," Max affirmed. "But they knew the address."

"We have to go back to Zelig," Chu announced.

Pro set her jaw. "I guess so."

Max turned to the two men. *"Ustedes regresen al trabajo. Gracias."*

The two men nodded and smiled and waved as Max and the detectives left.

Chu whispered to Pro, "He told them they could return to work and thanked them."

"I got the gist of it," Pro grumbled.

"How did you find those guys?" Chu asked as they made their way to the car.

"I went and asked that nice Ms. Irving if she saw the men who had replaced May's window. She described them and mentioned she'd seen them pouring concrete on 56th Street."

"You have the most damned luck," Pro fumed as they got into the car.

As Max got in the back, Chu looked in the mirror. "I don't recall inviting you along."

Max smiled. "It's okay, I'll text you the contact information for Tony and Jesus before we talk to this Zelig fellow."

"Max, you are interfering in an investigation," Pro sputtered.

"No, I'm not," Max protested. "I'm helping."

Chu took a deep breath. "Max, you are not part of the investigation. You can text me the contact information for Alvarez and Morales, but I would prefer you write up everything they told you in a statement."

"Like a report?" Max questioned.

"Yes, I think that would be the best use of your time," Chu said.

"I thought we could question the boss at the—"

By now Pro had gotten out of the car and pulled open the back door. "Max, get out!"

He looked up at her stunned but didn't move from the back seat.

"Don't make me call Mom!" she threatened.

Max slid across the seat and got out. "You guys used to be fun."

"No, Max, we are not fun, we are detectives. And asking you to look at a lock doesn't make you part of our 'team.' We are busy. Go find something to do."

Pro got in the car with Chu, and the detectives drove away as Max stood there.

"Hm," he said to himself. "Find something to do. I think I have an idea."

7. Banana-Bandada

Pro sat in the cafe waiting for Jamie, as nervous as she could be.

The day had not gone well. After leaving Max and returning to Zelig Construction, they found the office locked and Zelig gone. So, they went back to talk to any of the last of the witnesses the uniforms had found when canvassing the neighborhood.

The only good thing was that when they returned to the station, Max had emailed Chu a very detailed report of his interview with Alvarez and Morales. Looking it over, even Pro had to accept the fact that her father had done an excellent job.

It had also kept the old man out of their hair.

Finally closing down at 7:00, Pro had taken a quick shower in the precinct locker room before heading out to meet Jamie. And then she grew angry at herself for getting cleaned up as if she were going on a date.

But she kept reassuring herself that she "could do this." She arrived at the Magnolia Bakery location at 200 Columbus Avenue by 7:45.

Stepping into the store was nirvana. The smell of fresh-baked cookies and cupcakes wafted in the air, mixed with the scent of fruit pies and cakes. She ordered a cup of coffee and sat at one of the small round tables in a metal-backed chair. She looked longingly at the cupcakes and desperately wanted the banana pudding.

Growing up in NYC, the bakery was a special place Elisha had brought her when she wanted a treat. Back then, the only store was downtown on Bleecker Street. Sitting in this uptown location still took her back to when she was a little girl.

She recalled when she was about eight or nine and had just come home from visiting Max in Las Vegas. Max had remarried, and Trixie, his new wife, had an only slightly hidden contempt for Prophecy. In fact, she had overheard Trixie tell Max she didn't appreciate his "little brown mistake" coming to *her* house.

When Max had been there it was fine, but when he was off doing his show, and it was just her and Trixie in the spacious desert home, Pro remained alone in the guest room.

Trixie had worked in the show until she married Max, and then she found being on stage beneath her. Instead she walked around the large house—that could easily be called a mansion—in a semi-drunken stupor most of the time.

She had come out of the bedroom to get some snacks, walked into the kitchen, and found Trixie kissing a very good-looking young man.

She parted from him and turned to Pro to mutter, "The kid's here, dammit."

She got Pro's requested snacks and escorted her back to the guest room, recommending the young girl stay in there and "mind your own business," with a heavy warning that, "Max better not hear anything about this."

On coming home, Pro had tearfully told her mother the entire story, and her wise and patient mother had taken her by subway to the Magnolia Bakery. There, to raise her spirits, she bought a treat that combined vanilla pudding, fresh bananas, and vanilla wafer cookies in the mix.

It was then she told her mother she "didn't want to visit Daddy anymore."

"Lost in thought?" a voice with an Irish accent asked.

Pro started and looked up. It was Jamie. In her reverie, she hadn't even seen him come in the restaurant. She looked up at his red hair, his pale freckled skin, and was thankful they were in a public place.

"Sorry. Just thinking about one of the times I visited the bakery in the past."

He sat across from her. "And that memory made you look so sad."

"It was a rough one. My mother brought me here when I needed my spirits lifted," Pro clarified.

She sat there and wondered: *God, how could his eyes be that impossible shade of green?*

She could feel his desire for her as if it were the heat of a flame.

"What would ye like? It'll be my treat," he offered.

"Banana pudding, please," she said and felt her face flush.

He nodded. "I believe I'll have one of those wee cheesecakes."

He went to the counter and ordered as Pro looked out onto Columbus Avenue. The day had grown cooler, and with sunset falling just as she'd arrived here, the temperature would be cooler tonight. Even so, she could see the avenue easily with the numerous streetlights and endless headlights, keeping the roadway illuminated all night.

After a short time, Jamie returned with a white cardboard container with the requested pudding and a small round cheesecake on a plate for himself.

"How was your day?" he asked.

Pro was grateful she could look down at the food and avoid making eye contact with him. The delicacy was as good as she remembered it. The silken pudding with the squishy pieces of banana and the crunch of the cookies. "It's a double homicide, something to do with drugs. Killer sneaked in through a trick window."

"A trick window?" Jamie frowned, confused by this.

"Yeah, the window had security bars, but they'd been rebuilt with a catch on the outside. My father helped us find it."

"Your father? I thought you hadn't seen him in years."

"He showed up about six months ago. Now, he's moved in with my mother," Pro said and shook her head. She suddenly felt a twinge of guilt. She had not yet told Luther that her mom and dad were living together.

"I thought they had a messy divorce," Jamie said.

Pro lifted her eyes just as she put the spoon in her mouth, and Jamie was staring at her again, and she felt herself tremble.

"Look, Jamie," Pro sighed. "I only agreed to meet you tonight to tell you that I can't see you anymore. And you can't come by my place like you did."

"Why not?" he asked, almost flippantly.

"Because, I *am* seeing someone. Luther, that man from the other night."

He pushed out his lips to consider this. "Seemed like a nice sort. Didn't really think he was your type."

"He *is* my type," Pro protested. "In fact, he's exactly my type. *You* are the one who isn't my type."

A mischievous grin appeared on his face. "But we made it work, didn't we?"

She stared at her pudding, fuming. "No, we didn't make it work. Because you left."

He reached out and took her hand. "Pro, I didn't want to leave you."

"That doesn't matter," she snapped. "You did leave. In the end, you left me. And then, a few feeble attempts, and I didn't hear from you anymore."

She found she was breathing hard. Was it anger or desire? She really couldn't tell which, but she knew that she had spoken her truth. All the nights she spent alone, wanting him, needing him, but he had left, because magicians always leave.

At that moment, she glanced out the window and her blood went cold. On the other side of the glass stood Luther, staring at the pair of them. Jamie's hand lay on top of hers, and she had been gazing into Jamie's eyes as she'd spoken.

She jumped up and ran to the door, only to find that Luther had turned and began to walk away.

"Luther!" she called out and followed him. "It's not what you think."

The big man stopped and turned to face her. He was angry but had complete control over himself. He spoke in a calm voice, "Lady, I don't play that."

"I'm not playing at anything, Luther," Pro said with tears in her eyes.

"I saw how you looked at him," was his only response.

She wanted to reach out and hug Luther but felt she couldn't. "I was breaking up with him."

"So, you've been seeing him?"

"No, no, that's not what I meant," Pro attempted.

Luther eyed her sadly. "You've helped me, Pro. I think I can make some decisions I've been putting off." He turned and walked away into the dark streets.

Pro stood as he went and tried to understand what he'd just said. It was cryptic, and she didn't know what he'd meant.

Finally, she turned and trudged back to the restaurant. She returned to the table, and Jamie watched her warily.

"I'm sorry," Jamie finally said. "Was that my fault?"

"Yes," Pro mumbled as she sat down. "And no. It was my own fault. I let you confuse me."

"Pro I never meant to do anything—"

Pro glared at him with fire in her eyes. "No, you never mean to do anything. Men like you, like my father, you just show up and turn everybody else's lives upside down."

Jamie glanced around the room as Pro had gotten rather loud. "I only wanted to see you."

Pro spoke quieter but intensely. "I know. And you did it with no regard to the changes in my life over the last year and a half. I'm a detective now, and I have cases to solve. Beyond that, I have...or had...a boyfriend. The thing I don't have time for is you showing up out of the blue."

Pro pushed the spoon into her pudding as if she wanted to stab it, and picked up a huge mouthful and shoved it into her mouth, much to Jamie's surprise.

She chewed and gulped it down, and then tears stabbed her eyes. "You should go," she croaked, and pushed the cardboard container away from her.

"Is that what you want, Pro?"

Her jaw grew firm. "Yes, that's what I want."

He rose. "I do still love ye, Pro," he said. Then he walked out of the cafe without a look back.

Pro stared at the empty seat, then rose and threw out the remains of her pudding and returned Jamie's plate to someone behind a counter as if in a dream.

She stepped out onto Columbus Avenue and pulled out her smart phone to quickly text her mother: *Can I crash in my old room tonight? Upset.*

She started uptown and began to turn onto streets so she would reach West End Avenue. Her phone made a tone to tell her there was a new text: *No problem, honey. Do you need to talk?*

Pro considered this. Talk? Yeah, she'd talk about the fact that she'd just hurt the man she'd been dating for six months. Why had she agreed to meet Jamie? She knew it was nothing but trouble, and the worst possible scenario had come true. Luther saw them and assumed they were involved, and that Pro was dating other men.

She was going through mixed emotions: a part of her wanted to be angry. They weren't married. Hell, neither of them said they were exclusive. She was a single woman, and if she wanted to date other men, what was that to him?

But on the other hand, she felt they had both just accepted the idea that if they were dating, it *would* be exclusive. Neither of them had the time to spare in the pursuit of others.

These concepts battled through her mind as she made her way west and north until she reached her mother's—and now Max's—condo. She took the elevator up and knocked at the door out of respect, even though she had a key.

Max pulled the door open. "Pumpkin," he bellowed.

Pro stomped past him. "I am *not* your pumpkin! I am nobody's freakin' pumpkin."

She reached the center of the room and looked at her mother, who was sitting and watching television. The older woman turned off the screen with a remote as Pro drew near, and rose to hug her daughter. "What happened, baby?"

"Men!" she bellowed. "They all suck!"

"I'm going out for wine again," said Max as he headed out the door.

Once the door slammed, Pro hung her head and allowed a steady stream of salty tears to flow down her cheek, releasing the frustration she held inside. Through muffled sobs she told her mother the entire story, aware that the emotions alive within her were much stronger than she'd realized.

Once she finished, Elisha sat her at the table. "You want tea?"

"Got anything a little stronger?" Pro asked.

"Your father should be back in a few minutes with wine."

Pro rose to her feet again. "And him! He's doing it again, Mom. Showing up to question witnesses before we get there, inserting himself in my case."

Elisha frowned. "He told me that Tom asked for his help."

"For one little thing, now he's making himself a part of the entire investigation!"

There was the sound of a key in the lock, and Max stepped in with a bottle in a paper sack. Both women crossed their arms and glared at him.

"I understand you've been pushing your way into our daughter's job," Elisha said with a cold tone to her voice.

Max glanced at his watch. "You know, now would be a great time to get ice cream."

He turned for the door, and Elisha barked, "Leave the wine."

Max placed the bottle on a nearby table and hotfooted it out the door.

Elisha walked over, grabbed the bottle, and came back to the kitchen to get a corkscrew. "Don't worry, I'll talk to Max and tell him to back off."

"Can't you tie him up or something?"

Elisha sighed as she pulled the cork. "I could, but you know he can escape from almost anything, right?"

Elisha poured herself and Pro each a glass of wine. Pro took it and gulped a huge mouthful. "You're supposed to savor it, honey."

"I'm after the effect," Pro answered.

"It won't fix things with Luther."

"I know," Pro sighed. "Mom, did you ever date two men?"

Elisha frowned. "I thought you weren't going to date Jamie."

"Nice attempt to avoid the question."

Elisha sipped her wine. "I do try. But, to answer your question, yes. If you want to know the whole sordid truth, I actually dated three men at the same time, and slept with all of them."

Pro's mouth fell open. "Momma!"

"Oh hush! Don't look so shocked. How was I going to know who I really wanted to be with if I didn't check?"

"Did you run into problems? I mean, did anyone get jealous?"

"You think I let any of them know I was seeing the others? Hell no."

"What made you settle down?"

"I met your father." Elisha smirked. "After our first date, I broke up with the others the next day."

"So counting Max you were dating *four* men?"

"No, because after I met Max, he was the only one I wanted to spend time with." Elisha smiled at her daughter. "Back then, he was a force of nature, and I was completely smitten as he was with me. We couldn't get enough of each other, in life and especially in bed."

"Don't need to hear that part, Mom." Pro scowled.

Elisha shook her head, lost in the memory. "Max was already a success then. After all, he was ten years my senior. But, I had just started my business, and he gave me the freedom to focus on it. That's when we got married and got this place and had you."

"What about after the divorce?" Pro said.

Elisha grew serious. "Well, that was different because I had you, and I couldn't be a silly kid anymore. When Joe asked me out, we took things slow, and it was only when I knew that he was gonna stay around that I even let him meet you."

"He was a great man, Mom."

"Yes, he was, and he loved you as much as your father. But don't tell Max that."

Pro grimaced. "Max has always loved Max more than anyone else."

"Don't sell him short, honey. Your father would do anything to make you happy."

"Except stay off my cases."

"He's bored and trying to find himself. A career change at his age is tough. He doesn't need money, but he needs to find something to do."

The key turned in the lock again, and a large white silk handkerchief waved in the doorway. Max called out, "Truce?"

"You're safe enough," Elisha said. "Until I get you alone and give you a piece of my mind."

Max came in the door with the paper bag in front of him. "You don't want to hurt me; I have ice cream."

Elisha smiled in spite of herself, as Pro huffed out an exasperated breath.

8. Dagger Head Box

Pro woke up in the small bedroom in which she had spent her childhood. It was now a guest room, and the many toys, stuffed animals, and boy band posters were long gone.

But the room still wore pink drapes and a pink bedspread. Pro got out of bed in a pair of pajamas her mother always had in a drawer in case she stayed over. They were also pink.

Pro shook her head. "I can't believe I was so girly growing up," she muttered. The pink drapes and bedspread certainly wouldn't suit the Spartan apartment she had in Brooklyn. And to Pro that made sense. She was a kick-ass detective and didn't have time for "girly" things anymore.

So why was she getting so confused about Jamie and Luther? She had made a decision, and Jamie was out. Now, she would have to fix things with Luther and get back to her life.

She threw on a robe and came out to get coffee. The machine her mother had in the kitchen was one of those things that used little plastic cups, and Pro frowned as she tried to make it work.

"I'll get that for you, pumpkin," Max said as he pushed past her, opened the device, shoved in a container of coffee, and set the machine to gurgling with a cup underneath.

"Thanks, and don't call me pumpkin," she said without getting mad.

"You might want to consider calling me 'Dad' again."

"Don't push it, Max," Pro objected. "We have a ways to go before I'll be comfortable with that."

Max moved to the hall, again brushing past Pro in the room that was designed more like a hallway than an actual kitchen. He glanced out and returned to Pro. "What if I made it legal?"

"What are you talking about?" Pro complained, as the machine finished and she grabbed her mug and took a much needed sip.

Max reached into the robe he was wearing and pulled a small jewelry box out of his pocket.

"What's that?" Pro asked, immediately concerned.

"I want to ask your mother to marry me," Max said and opened the box to show an engagement ring. True to Max's style, the single diamond in the center was huge.

"Holy crap," Pro hissed. "That's not a ring; that's a weapon."

"Too much?" Max worried.

"Yes! Max, does Mom seem like a woman who would wear something that extravagant?"

His shoulders lowered. "I guess not."

"You got married to too many bimbos," Pro said. "Mom would want something reasonable that she could keep on her hand while she works." She blew out a breath. "Do you know her at all?"

"Are you two fighting already?" Elisha's voice came from the other room.

Max, completely unfazed, did something with his hands, and the ring and the box were gone.

Elisha stood in the doorway. "Somebody better make me coffee, or get the hell out of my way."

"I've got it, dear," Max said, and slid past Pro to get to the machine. His daughter took her coffee and went past her mother to go out to what they called the "dining room," which was a table just outside the kitchen.

She sipped and thought about it. Max wanted to propose? Would her mother say yes? The idea of her parents getting married again annoyed her, and yet, maybe it would be a good thing.

Last night, Elisha had told her how she and Max first got together. Doing the math in her head, she decided Elisha had been twenty-six when Pro had been born. Pro was now twenty-seven, and to her, marriage or babies seemed like a weird, foreign concept. Having babies was what other women did, not kick-ass detectives. The idea of her walking into bloody crime scenes with a huge belly was an image she pushed out of her head right away.

But the thought invaded her again, like an earwig trying to drill into her mind: *How would Luther feel about being a husband?* Then came the uninvited follow-up: *How would Jamie?*

She had a sudden desire to take her coffee and pour it over her own head, if only to make these thoughts go away.

She jumped up and shouted, "I'm taking a shower."

* * *

Arriving at the precinct an hour later, Pro breathed a sigh of relief. She was back where everything made sense. She could focus on the two puzzling cases and not have romance or boyfriends get into her head.

She texted Luther before she got on the subway, hoping that he had calmed down in the new morning. She had made it a rather long text, that she was just meeting with Jamie for old time's sake, and to explain that she was seeing Luther.

She decided this was the best tack, but in the walk to the precinct, she had not received a text back. She would call him later, once she knew he was on duty at the front desk of the condominium where he ran security.

Pro had enjoyed the six months with Luther, and the fact that she had a steady sex life. It might not have been as mind-blowing as her previous encounters with Jamie, but he did get the job done.

Oh yes.

She went to her desk to see Tom already at his station, working on the computer. "Hey, partner," she said as she sat. He looked up with a miserable expression. "You okay?"

"My parents had that girl over last night," he muttered. "Seo-yun Pak. She grew up in South Korea and moved here five years ago."

"Wow!" Pro declared. "I haveta tell you, partner, if you're going to break Julie's heart, I'm going to have to kick your ass."

This got a small smile which disappeared immediately. He spoke quietly. "Pro, I'm miserable. All I can think about is Julie. I had a terrible evening, but the girl wants to see me again."

"I can't say I blame her; you're quite the catch."

"Pro," he whined, "you're not helping."

"Don't look at me," Pro said. "As I see it, your situation is easy. You tell your parents, you buy a ring, end of problem."

Chu sighed.

"You think you got problems? Max wants to propose to my mom."

"How is that a problem?"

"Beside the fact that he bought her a ring with a diamond the size of a doorknob, it means he'll feel even more entitled to become part of our cases."

"He showed you the ring?"

Pro nodded as she pulled up files on her screen.

"Big diamond, huh?"

"It's just Max showing off. I hope he'll get her something reasonable. Or that my mom'll shoot him down."

Chu sighed again. "I think I may have found the book club that May went to."

Pro brightened. "Really? How?"

"The first team found a flyer advertising it, and it was in with the evidence from the scene. Crime Scene Team found the same flyer at James' apartment."

"Impressive. Where are they?"

Chu hit a key and a link to the website was messaged to her. She hit the link and it opened to a web page that showed books and some cutesy graphics of cats sitting on books or walking around the page with the masthead:

CHELSEA BOOK CLUB
It's the cat's meow

Pro looked at Chu with a raised eyebrow. "You gotta be kidding me."

"So you found the book club," a voice came from behind her.

"Max, you don't need to be here," Pro announced without looking back.

Her father leaned forward and gazed at the screen. "Look, the meeting is tonight."

Pro stood, folded her arms, and looked down at her father as he leaned against her desk. "And we can handle going there and asking questions."

"Oh yeah," Max mocked, "and the drug dealers who just took out two of their operatives will just tell you their scheme. Come on, Pro, you need someone who can get in there and be accepted."

"That's ridiculous, Max. Tom and I are trained to handle situations just like this."

Max shook his head. "Yeah, you're right. You fit right in with a fifty-year-old like May Johnson, or the guy who was knifed, Thomas James. How old was he, Tom?"

Tom had risen from his chair and joined them. "Forty."

"See," Max said triumphantly. "I could go undercover into the group and find out who is moving this stuff and who killed James and Johnson."

Pro's expression grew hard. "Max, the NYPD has trained people to work undercover—"

"And they wouldn't fool anyone. Come on, I read the report of May's broken neck, and the knife attack that killed James. These guys have a professional on their team, and they would be able to smell a cop. I'm the perfect choice! I have the acting training and enough of a wardrobe to—"

"Absolutely not!" Pro snapped.

"Pro, hold on," Tom considered. "Maybe he's on to something."

"We could be dealing with killers, even if they masquerade as a book club," Pro argued.

"But he might be able to find out more than we could," Chu said. "Think about it. We put a wire on him, and we have surveillance—"

"You can't possibly believe this is a good idea—"

"Pro," Max said, "I've been deceiving people my entire life. This is just another illusion."

"And what if someone decides he's a threat and takes him out?" Pro queried. "How would I explain that to my mother?"

"I'll just make the initial contacts and then turn the case over to you two," Max offered. "I can get names, and you stick a camera on me, you can get photos of them."

"There should be very little danger with that, Pro," Tom said. "Let me talk to the captain, see if he'll go along with it."

"You've made up your mind," Pro grumbled. "What choice do I have?"

Tom smiled and headed out of the bullpen to speak to the captain.

"So, you did it," Pro fumed. "You pushed yourself into *my* case!"

"I'm only trying to help, Pro."

"Well, if you get yourself killed, I'm never speaking to you again."

"Outside of a séance, anyway."

* * *

The captain did approve the idea and told Chu that he hoped Max would tell his good friend the mayor of the precinct's willingness to try something different.

Lieutenant Dunton also liked the concept, perhaps because he was still sore at Max's escape from a holding cell six months earlier and liked the idea of Max having to follow orders for a change.

But a lot of the day was spent getting Max a tiny camera and instructing him on the use of the wire. Chu also had to arrange an NYPD surveillance vehicle.

Meanwhile, Pro continued to interview people who lived in the two buildings where the murders occurred, as someone had to do the actual police work. The witnesses seemed to know very little. The resident in the apartment directly above Thomas James was not even aware that anything had happened. The pair of hearing aids the older man wore seemed to suggest why he'd missed the ruckus.

She also attempted to call Mr. Zelig, but no one answered the phone. She went by his office, but it was closed and it looked like no one had come by.

Going to the place where the construction team had been the previous day, she found no workers there, but the cement had hardened nicely.

She texted Luther between stops, and still had not received a reply. Finally, she gave in and stopped by the condo, which was only a few blocks south of the work site.

Pro headed into the lobby, which was decorated completely in white, even the couches and pots for plants. A large white desk was watched by two men in blue suit jackets with matching ties. One was a skinny man with dark hair that Pro knew as Jorge and had seen numerous times when she met Luther after work, or going up to his apartment in the building. The other was a tall Caucasian man with broad shoulders that Pro had never seen before.

Pro walked up to the desk and Jorge's eyes lit up.

"Oh, hey, Pro," he said shyly.

"Hi, Jorge," Pro said, eyeing the newcomer. "I thought Luther would be on this afternoon."

"Sure, come with me, let's talk," Jorge said.

This was unusual, but Pro followed him into a little side room through a white door. This was where the security officers had a locker room and break room. Pro had been in it many times when she visited Luther at work and they needed to talk and go over plans. In the room, a bank of small televisions displayed different views of the lobby and front door, and Pro knew that they were recording video in case anything happened. The system had been put in after the murder of a resident six months earlier and the need for heightened security.

"He's gone," Jorge told her as they stepped into the room.

"Gone?" Pro repeated. "What do you mean, he's gone?"

"The company offered Luther a special assignment, and he kept turning them down. Then last night, he starts calling everyone to let them know he's taken it. He said he had to leave this morning."

Pro stared at Jorge. "Where did he go?"

He shrugged. "I don't know, Pro. I thought you might know what it was about."

Pro felt as if the floor had fallen away and she was floating. "No, I don't...um...thanks, Jorge," she finally stammered, and then without another word walked out of the room and then out of the building, heading back to the precinct.

She couldn't understand it. He just left, just like that. One little disagreement and he'd flown off the handle and literally flew away.

Suddenly, the shock was gone as anger replaced it. What kind of relationship did they have if one little thing like her having a snack with an old boyfriend made him run away like a scared little girl? How dare he presume? How could he have so little respect for her, for them?

A thought occurred to her, that it would serve him right if she *had* bedded Jamie. At least then he'd have something real to be angry about. And even then, what right did he have? They weren't married, and if he had so little respect for her...

She pulled out her phone and texted the new number she had for Jamie: *If you want to get together tonight is good, but it will be late.*

A few seconds went by, but there was a rapid reply: *Am confused. But will meet you anywhere, anytime.*

She tapped at the virtual keyboard: *My place, 11:00.*

She jammed the phone back into her pocket. She'd show Luther. If he was going to run off like that, she'd replace him. She had not been intimate with Luther recently, and since she had an itch, Jamie would be the one to scratch it.

She stormed back to the precinct and made plans in her head for the night, while debating with herself about how she and her partner should handle Max.

9. Brainwave Deck

The Chelsea Book Club met at the Chelsea Piers Sports & Entertainment Complex. This was a twenty-eight acre waterfront sports and catering establishment located between 17th and 23rd Streets along Manhattan's Hudson River. They had meeting rooms and sports facilities of all sizes transformed from four long-ignored piers into a major center for public recreation and waterfront access. The book club met in a small meeting room on the second floor at Pier 60.

At 7:15, the NYPD surveillance vehicle pulled into the large parking lot of the correct pier directly in front of the building.

The driver was also the technician and a detective named Michael Hayes. He was a thin Caucasian man with a full head of brown hair and a mustache. He came around to the back of the overlong van to get Max set up with the tiny camera he would wear on his jacket. With that and a 'wire' the police would get audio and video of the attendees at the meeting.

As Hayes taped the thin microphone cord to Max's bare chest, Pro looked over Max's disguise. He was wearing horn-rimmed glasses and had parted his hair down the middle in a way that made it fall into his face. Pro had to admit, it made him look nerdy and very different from the suave stage persona he usually projected.

Once the body pack transmitter was in his back pocket and the wire in place and secured, Max put his shirt back on. It was a plaid one, to which he added a tweed jacket and a bowtie.

Chu exchanged a glance with Pro and lifted his eyebrows, impressed by Max's transformation.

With the jacket in place, Detective Hayes placed the camera and went over the do's and don'ts with Max. "Don't try to manipulate the camera; you can't. Just talk to people and look straight at them. The lens should catch anyone you talk to. For the best image, you want to be about three to five feet away."

Max nodded. Pro knew that Max had a strong memory as he did mentalism in his magic show that required remarkable memorization. Max could glance at a paper and write down the salient points and even numbers weeks later.

"Okay," Tom added. "You don't go anywhere but the meeting and then you come right back here. Got it?"

"Of course, detective," Max assured, using the official title since Hayes was there.

"Now, let me give you the earpiece," Hayes affirmed. "You know how to use one, right?"

"I've been using one in my act for years," Max said as Hayes handed him the small device. "I have to tell you mine is smaller."

"Yes, and the quality is probably better. But that one is designed to look like a hearing aid. So, in your case, it shouldn't attract any suspicion."

"Thank you for reaffirming that I look old, detective." Max smirked.

Chu broke in. "So, we can hear you through the wire, and you can hear us through the earpiece, got it?"

"I feel safer already."

"Max, if you ever want to work with us again, it means that if I give you an order, you obey it," Chu commanded.

"Without question, detective," Max replied.

"Wish I could believe that," Pro muttered.

Chu checked his watch. "It's time."

Hayes escorted Max to the rear door, opened it, and Max stepped out, with a wink to Pro as he went.

Pro shook her head. "I can't believe the captain and the LT agreed to this."

"He's going to a meeting for an hour or so. What could happen?"

"With Max?" Pro whined. "Almost anything."

Hayes put on headphones with an attached microphone and moved to a monitor fastened to a bank of machinery in the van's cargo space.

Max walked in the parking lot and turned into a small room that contained two elevators and stairs. He carried a copy of a book called *The Muse*. It was published by Brain Bender Press, and Max had found a duplicate at a book store. It was the same as one of the "gimmicked" books they'd found at May Johnson's house. If the title of the book was some kind of code, it might encourage a member of the gang to make contact.

If they were even there.

Max rode up in the huge elevator one floor and exited into a hallway. He took a right following a sign to "Meeting Rooms" and strode by several closed ones, until he found the one that had a paper sign out front that was scrawled by hand with "Chelsea Book Club."

He stepped into the room which had about a dozen people milling about. The room had an open space near the door where the people currently congregated. Deeper in the room, the chairs had been arranged in a "theatre style" layout. Two chairs with a table between them were in the front, which faced several rows of chairs that were the "audience." A large cardboard box rested under the table with the lid closed.

Max figured the attendees, including himself, would sit in the "audience" section and that whoever was running the show would be in the front.

"You're not wearing a name tag," said a sultry voice. Max turned to see a woman in her forties with flaming-red hair speaking to him.

"I'm sorry, I'm new," Max said, trying to keep his voice high so he sounded nerdy.

"Haven't you been here before?" she asked. The woman was in a one-piece outfit with flared sleeves and equally flared hems of the pants. But it fit tightly against every curve of her body, and the curves were quite something to look at.

But Max remained in character. "No, first time, really."

"But you brought the book we're currently reading," she said and put her hand on Max's book, but he kept a firm grip on it.

"Yes, I wanted to be up to speed, as it were," he said, trying to be polite.

She smiled and dusted off Max's shoulder as if there had been something on it. "Well, get a name tag. They are right over there." She pointed at a small table near the door with a perfectly manicured finger —with red nail polish, of course.

Max nodded and made his way to the table, taking one more glance back to watch the woman's posterior as she strode away.

"Keep it in your pants, Max," Pro's voice chided through the earpiece.

Max wanted to say something back, but he instead moved to the small table. There he put the book down and wrote the false name "Manny Heller" on a label and stuck the adhesive paper to the lapel of his jacket just below where the camera was located. This way if anyone got close to see his name, they would get a good view of the person's face.

A man picked up the book as it lay on the table and took an admiring look at it. "I see you have our most recent club choice," he said. The man was only slightly shorter than Max's six-foot-four and was dressed in a "power" suit that suggested he was with a Wall Street firm or some other high-powered office. He had a full head of dark hair and a strong chin with a dimple in it.

He held out his hand. "Hi, I'm Edward Mandel. I'm the one who put this little group together."

Max shook his hand. "I'm Manny. My, you don't *look* like a fellow who likes books."

Mandel gave a movie-star quality smile. "Books are my job. But I like to get out and meet the people who actually read them." He flipped the book over in his hand and skimmed through the pages. "How far are you into the book?"

"Only the first third," Max lied. "Still getting to know the characters."

"You're going to have to do better than that if you want to become a member," Mandel confided. "We go through a book this size every week."

People began to get into seats, and Mandel looked up to the front of the room where the red-haired woman sat at one of the chairs that faced the group.

"I have to join Elena," Mandel said, and handed Max the book as he headed for the front of the room.

"We're going to run him," Pro's voice mentioned in his earpiece. He didn't bother to say anything, as it seemed Pro had things in hand. He knew that "run him" meant they would look him up in the police database.

The meeting was called to order, and Max found his way to a seat, making sure to slowly turn his body so that the camera caught all of the people in the room. He had to admit that many of them did not look like book lovers. Several were large men with shaved heads and a glare that Max had only seen in the eyes of criminals. They monitored the room carefully, like a pride of predators. But mixed into the group were several older people who seemed harmless, unlike the rough men who sat as a group away from the other participants.

He finally moved up to the first row, where he decided the camera wouldn't be blocked by any bodies, and took a seat.

The red-haired woman stood. "Welcome to the Chelsea Book Club. Most of you know I am Elena Byrne, the president of the club, and next to me is Ed Mandel, the founder. We wanted to have an open discussion about this week's selection."

The next forty-five minutes were spent discussing the various pros and cons of the book, which apparently was a horror novel where a famed writer was possessed by a creature that helped him write but transformed him into a serial killer.

Looking over the room, Max noted that the group of hard young men sitting apart from the others listened attentively but offered nothing. The rest of the attendees were fortyish and fiftyish people who commented with many insights into the dark tale.

Max could see that the older women adored Edward, and every time the man spoke, it was like a sigh went through the room.

Max studied the cadre of men in the corner as they sat with their arms folded. Any one of them looked like they had the ability to break May's neck or use a knife on Thomas James. From the look of several of them, they might even enjoy it.

He also considered that Edward and Elena had both shown an interest in touching his copy of *The*

Muse, but neither had done or said anything that might suggest they were a part of a drug crime ring.

Finally, as the meeting drew to a close, Edward pulled out the box that had been under a table and announced this week's read. He held up a book where the jacket was adorned with a knight on horseback and had the name *Last Knight* in bold letters.

There was a sticky note on it with a name that Edward removed and handed to Elena to show off the cover. She mentioned that the book was written by someone named Godwine, who was known for historic adventure novels.

From his seat, Max could see the telltale "brain" logo on the spine of the book. It had also been published by Brain Bender Press, just like the "special" ones that were hollowed out to hold drugs.

After praising it highly, she stuck the note with the name back in place and she and Edward began to lay out the books on the table and put the box on the floor in front of it.

"You all know the drill," Elena said. "Members get a free copy of the book and leave the book they just finished in the box."

"If you are a guest," Edward said, but he didn't look at Max, "you only get a free book once you join."

The large, tough men moved to the front and headed up to be the first to put their copy of *The Muse* in the box and grab a hardcover version of *Last Knight*. They each looked over the books on the table until they located the one that had a sticky note with their name on it.

Max muttered into the microphone, "I gotta get a look inside one of those books."

"Not your job, Max," Chu stated.

"I'll figure it out," Max said and stood. Others were standing and milling about in the back of the room where no chairs were in the way.

The men got their books and just left, not staying to socialize. However, an older woman went up to receive her book and held it to her chest protectively as others moved to the front of the room to get theirs.

She looked harmless enough, so Max approached her. "Hi, I'm Manny."

The woman all but jumped as she looked up at Max who was so much taller than her. She glared up at him as if he'd just appeared out of nowhere.

"Sorry, I wasn't trying to scare you," Max told her.

She eyed him with suspicion and held her book more tightly. "You shouldn't sneak up on people like that."

"Didn't mean to sneak," Max dismissed, and reached out for the book, trying to sound nonchalant. "Can I take a look at this? It looks like a fun read."

"Max, don't do that," Chu snapped over his earpiece.

"I told you this would happen," Pro complained.

The woman looked horrified as Max reached out and put a firm hand on the book. He gently attempted to pull it away, but the woman gave a screech and yanked the book away from Max. However, her grip was not solid on the book either, and it flew out of both of their hands and into the air. It flipped over once and fell to the floor.

At this point, every eye in the room was focused on the book as it landed on its spine and slid on the linoleum floor, until it hit the wall, at which point the tome fell open, exposing the interior of the book.

Max stared at it and turned his body so that the camera could face the spot where the book came to rest.

But as the book fell open, the only thing within it was the printed pages.

10. Penetration Pen

Later that night, Pro was almost back at her apartment, and was as nervous as she'd ever been in her life.

Getting Max out of the book club and back into the van, Pro was glad to see Tom chew out her father.

"I told you not to bother with the books," Tom exploded. "It was reconnaissance, nothing more. I just wanted to get some faces and names and run them. Now you made them suspicious."

"I don't think so," Max defended.

"You don't? Come on, Max! If the club is involved, those in the drug ring know that the drugs are in the books. You were interested in a member's book. They have to know you're working with the police."

They finally were driven by Detective Hayes back to the precinct, and Chu and Hayes wanted to get to work on the video the next day to analyze the names from the name tags and see if anyone popped.

Pro escorted Max out of the van.

Her father looked a bit sheepish. "Sorry if I didn't handle that right. I had a hunch and went with it."

"It was a bad move. What if it had been a gimmicked book full of drugs?" Pro questioned.

"Then I would hope that you and Tom would come get me out."

She stared at him deadpan.

"You would…wouldn't you?" Max fretted.

"I'm thinking…" Pro warned.

Finally, though, Max was sent home and Pro headed to her place in Brooklyn.

Now, as she walked up the stairs, she was a nervous wreck. She had asked Jamie over when she was angry at Luther, but the long day had chilled her temper. Suddenly, she was unsure of what she was planning to do.

In fact, she felt guilty…and she hadn't even done anything yet.

The idea went through her mind that she should text Jamie and cancel. But was that fair to him? If he was there and Luther was gone, maybe she could be with Jamie for the six months he stayed in America.

Why was this all so confusing?

As she reached the top stair, she found that Jamie was outside her door once again.

"How do you keep doing that?" Pro said, unhappy that she sounded so annoyed.

He gave her a dazzling smile. "I kept the key to the outer door ye gave me as a souvenir."

She frowned and came over to unlock the apartment door. "That explains why I couldn't find it after you left."

"I didn't know it would come in so handy."

He put his hand on her shoulder, and Pro shrugged it off.

"I should get it back from you," Pro said as they stepped into the apartment.

"Are ye feeling all right? Ye look tired."

Pro went in and turned on the standing lamp in the living room. "I've had a long day. My dad went undercover and it almost became a thing."

"I'm sorry," Jamie puzzled, as confusion darkened his features. "I thought your father was a magician?"

"Do you want some wine?" Pro asked and stepped into the closet that was her kitchen. "I need some wine."

"Sure," Jamie said and watched her as he went over to the padded chair and sat.

Pro poured two jelly jars of white wine from the bottle in the refrigerator, and stepped into the living room to give Jamie a glass.

He smiled. "This brings back memories." He took a sip.

Pro moved to the sofa, as memories flashed through her mind as well. Her memories were more carnal in nature, which surprised her.

She attempted to change the subject. "I was hoping to get a shower before you got here."

He snickered. "We could take one together."

She smiled in spite of herself. "Remember the time we tried that?"

He nodded. "That shower stall barely had enough room for us to stand side by side."

"And you wanted to make love, and there just wasn't enough room."

"I had to bloody pick ye up and use the wall for support," he laughed.

Pro flushed as the memory of that session flooded back into her mind. It had been almost impossible for them to push their bodies together, but once they'd joined, it had been very, very good.

Luther had once picked her up like that during lovemaking, and it had excited her. But he did weights, and his arms were so strong—

Where had that come from?

Pro was shocked that in the middle of remembering that shower scene with Jamie, a memory of Luther inserted its way in.

Jamie was sipping his wine and looking at her as if she was the most beautiful thing on the planet. She could feel his eyes undressing her, remembering each supple curve.

Luther never looked at her like that. He always looked at her as an equal, and he was always so controlled.

She slugged back the wine and wanted another, then kicked off her shoes and sighed at the relief it gave her.

Jamie put his glass aside, and picked up one of her legs.

"Oh, no," Pro whined. "I'm all sweaty and I—"

Her words stopped in her throat as Jamie began to massage her tired, aching foot.

"Oh my," Pro moaned. It was all she could manage. The foot rub seemed to touch nerves that traveled up her leg and made every erogenous zone on her body vibrate in anticipation.

Jamie pulled her other foot to his lap and now was kneading both of them with his clever hands.

"You looked troubled, Pro," he said as he continued to knead. "What's on your mind?"

What's on my mind, Pro thought, *is that I want to make love to you and that I am nothing more than a cheater.*

Pro pulled her feet away, sat up straight, and fought to maintain control. "This was a bad idea, Jamie."

"Was it now?"

She nodded sadly. "Luther—"

"Ah! The boyfriend."

"After he saw us last night, he left town and I got mad and I wanted...I wanted..."

"To show him ye didn't need him?"

Pro felt her lower lip tremble. "Yeah."

He moved to kneel in front of her and take her hand. "Pro, I came because ye asked. But I don't want to take advantage of ye."

"I know," Pro said, and a tear trailed down her face. "I'm just so confused. Everything was fine until I saw you..."

He leaned back and lifted an eyebrow. "So, it's my fault, is it?"

"No," Pro blurted. "Or yes. I don't know. It's just you brought up a lot of feelings I didn't know I still had."

"Or things you weren't sure about in your relationship with Luther."

Pro rose. She had to create space between them. He was being so considerate, which was so damn sexy, and looking into his eyes caused her brain to shut down and other longings to become far too active. It had been over two weeks since she had made love, and her body betrayed her in the fact that it was ready, even if her mind was not.

She rose and went to the refrigerator to refill her wine. Another thought pushed through: *Yeah, get drunk, then you don't have to take responsibility. You can screw the old boyfriend and blame it on the booze.*

She wanted to yell out, "Shut up," but she knew that wouldn't help.

Pro returned to the sofa and was glad that Jamie had moved back to the chair.

"I'm sorry I made you come all the way out here," she told him as she took a sip.

"The subways run all night," he assured her.

She stared at her glass. "I guess this wasn't the reception you expected."

"Not the one I would have preferred."

"Where are you staying?"

"I have a sublet in Alphabet City," Jamie told her, referring to the East Village section of Manhattan below 14th Street that consisted of avenues A, B, C, and D and was famous for artists living there.

"Wow, Manhattan. I couldn't afford that," Pro said, trying to get things back to a conversational tone.

"I told you, I've got a sponsor. They are willing to pay for me to do shows all over the world. I only have to finish writing me magic book first."

This made her giggle, or was it the wine? "I didn't know you were writing a book."

"Aye, and a big one, too. Me sponsor wants it to be this great big book all about street magic."

Pro's mouth twisted up in one corner. "You *do* know about that."

"Aye, it's a worldwide publisher. They tol' me they could get the book into stores all over the world."

"Do you have to pay them?" Pro said, knowing of vanity book companies that made authors pay large sums up front.

"No, they're payin' me expenses. It's a company called Brain Bender Press," he remarked as he took another sip of wine.

Pro's head snapped up, and she was suddenly stone-cold sober. "It's called…what?"

"Brain Bender Press. They're based in South America, I think. But they have representatives in the States and the UK, and the—"

Pro stood. "Jamie, you have to come to the precinct tomorrow."

Jamie was taken aback. "Why, am I under arrest or something?"

Pro shook her head to try to clear it. "No, the company you're talking about, Brain Bender Press? We found a book they published at a crime scene that contained opioids."

Jamie frowned. "That's ridiculous, Pro. I've been to their offices."

"But they want a big book, right?" Pro said as a realization came to her. "All of their books are big. That way they can fit more drugs."

"Pro, you're not making any sense."

"No, but it is beginning to make sense to me. Worldwide distribution, boxes of books, no one would question them."

"You saying I shouldn't write the book? I'm more than half done."

Pro rose. "No, I'm saying you should go back to your place, and come to my precinct tomorrow. Make it about ten. Don't speak to anyone but me or Detective Chu!"

"If that's what ye want," he said, flustered.

"Yes, this could be the first break we've gotten," Pro gloated, and Jamie could see she was excited by the possibilities.

He polished off the wine in one gulp and stood. "Very well, then. I hope you'll explain things more when I get there, because I'm a wee bit confused right now."

"Hopefully, I'll know more then," Pro said and walked to the door and opened it. "See you tomorrow."

He stepped into the hall, turned, and moved close. Pro was surprised by this, and then his lips met hers.

The acceleration of Pro's heart rate made a pounding in her ears, as she knew this was what she had really craved. She pulled away to stare at him, and with a gentle finger, Jamie reoriented her face so that he held her gaze. Every part of her was on fire, and she felt she wanted, needed to be touched. She wanted this man to use his clever fingers and talented tongue, then become one with her to take her to the place her body ached to go.

"I don't want to leave," he told her, his voice heavy, his breathing fast.

"I don't want you to go, either," she confessed.

He leaned to her and brought his lips to her neck, kissing and nuzzling her.

The same way Luther did.

She pushed Jamie away so fast, the man might've fallen over, but he quickly got his feet under him.

"I...can't..." she blurted and stepped back into the apartment. She stared at him, her eyes heavy with desire, but she forced herself to close the door and turn the locks.

She lowered herself to the floor and leaned against the door until she finally heard him walk down the stairs, his footfalls fading into the background noise of the traffic.

She slowly got up and pulled out the bed, and then got her glass and refilled it one last time. As she undressed, she looked at her empty fold-out bed and recalled a night with Luther not long ago.

They had been lying in the semi-darkness of this room, reflected light from street-lights slanting through the venetian blinds in the window.

They both lay on the bed naked, with Luther next to her, his skin so much darker than her own and his bald head shining with sweat from their efforts. It was one of the few times he came to her place, as his apartment in Manhattan was so much more convenient.

He leaned up on his elbows and looked at her. "You're one hell of a woman, Pro," he told her as his hand gently stroked her breast.

She smiled up at him, sated. "You're not bad yourself, Mr. Ardoin."

"So formal? Didn't I just 'get it on' with you?"

"Was that you?" Pro joked. "I was busy."

This made Luther give his big laugh. Jamie had a sexy laugh, but Luther's was big, loud, and from the belly.

They lay side by side in silence for a moment.

"So where are we going with this, girl?" Luther finally said.

"To a place where you stop calling me 'girl,' I hope."

"C'mon, Pro, I'm serious. I like you. I think you like me. Maybe we ought to think about taking this to the next level."

But that was it and Pro knew it. She did "like" Luther, and Luther did "like" her. That was the problem. "Like" was the only L-word Luther had used.

Never love.

And a part of her held back because she couldn't be the first to say it. It was too hard, because the men in her life always left. Max flew off to Vegas, Joe died, and Jamie had gone back to Ireland.

But did she love Luther? That was hard to say as well.

If she truly loved him, would she be rubbing up against her old boyfriend and wanting him so bad it made her eyes water, as well as other parts? But, if she didn't love him, why had thoughts and memories of Luther interrupted what could have been a night of passion with Jamie?

Pro got under the covers, longing to be held, to be touched. She hated that she'd sent Jamie away, and at the same time wished Luther was in the bed with her.

She rolled around in the bed like a cat in heat, and finally got up, poured the last of her wine, drank it, and fell asleep in an alcohol haze.

11. Square Circle

As she walked up the Midtown North Precinct stairs to the bullpen, coffee in hand, Pro had a craving to just throw herself down the stairs and end it all. Maybe then her head wouldn't be pounding, and it would end the painfully bright light coming in the windows, even though she wore sunglasses on her face.

She went to her desk, hardly looking up as Chu asked her, "Rough night?"

She sat with a sigh and grumbled, "I'd better figure out this guy thing, or I'm going to end up an alcoholic."

Chu frowned. "I thought you had decided what to do?"

"I did," Pro complained. "And then Luther saw me when I was talking to Jamie and left town. I got mad and invited Jamie over."

Chu looked confused trying to follow this. "So, you're seeing Jamie?"

"Actually," Pro sighed, "we both are."

Now Tom was really confused. "What?"

She leaned forward on her desk. "Jamie has this sponsor that wants him to write a magic book."

"Good for him. So what?"

"It's Brain Bender Press."

Chu's head shot up, rather like Pro's the previous night. "The same publisher as the gimmicked books?"

"You got it. I asked Jamie to come by so we could ask him about it, and maybe get a name of someone in the New York office."

Chu considered this. "You think maybe this drug thing is bigger than just the book club?"

"Think about it, Tom. You can ship books all over the world, and who would check a box of books?"

Chu nodded. "If this is a possibility, we'll have to bring in the Drug Enforcement Agency."

"You can bring in the Boy Scouts, for all I care, as long as we work the murder. Any luck on Edward Mandel?"

"No police record that I could find. Maybe we should look him up on Google."

"I'm on it," Pro said, and went to the browser on her computer and started a search. Fortunately, she could recall the correct spelling of his name after seeing his name tag on camera the previous evening.

A lot of people with his name came up: several CEOs; a teacher; a video producer; the list went on.

On a whim, Pro typed in the name and followed it with "Brain Bender Press," which led her to a page with a bio.

"Listen to this," Pro gushed. "Edward Mandel is the President of United States operations for Brain Bender Press."

"What?" Chu said, so surprised that he walked around the facing desks to look at her screen. On it was a photo of the man they saw last night, on one of the Brain Bender Press web pages. It was a collection of different people, and the top of the page had a masthead that read "Our Staff."

"Wait." Chu pointed at the computer. "Scroll down!"

Pro used the mouse and maneuvered down the page, where a photo of the previous evening's redhead appeared. Next to the photo the header read:

Elena Byrne:
Vice President of United States Operations

Chu whistled. "Well, this is looking very suspicious."

"Detectives?" Jacobs, a tall uniformed officer, called out as he stuck his head into the bullpen. "There's someone who was told to come in and see you?"

"Irish guy, Jacobs?" Chu asked.

The lanky officer nodded.

"Put him in an interview room, not in interrogation," Chu ordered. "We'll be there soon."

"Will do, detective," Jacobs said and left.

Pro glanced at her watch. Jamie had not only come in as she'd asked, he'd arrived early.

"I'll call the contractor," Pro suggested.

"And maybe we need to take a visit to the offices of Brain Bender Press."

Pro smiled. "I would like that. Catch Mandel and Byrne when they aren't expecting it."

They both got on phones, Pro to the contractor, and Chu to the main number for the publisher.

Pro got an answering machine and left a message: " Zelig, it's Detective Pro Thompson with NYPD. I need to speak to you again." She then left her cell number and hung up.

Tom, however, seemed to be getting the runaround from whoever he spoke to at Brain Bender Press when he requested to speak to either Edward Mandel or Elena Byrne.

Pro took this opportunity to go to the interview room, where Jamie waited patiently behind the scuffed table that separated him from her.

Good, she thought as she sat down. *I need something between the two of us.*

Pro sat across from her former lover and was all business. "Thank you for coming in, Mr. Tobin. My partner and I will have some questions for you about your arrangement with Brain Bender Press. Can I get you anything?"

"No, I'm fine, Pro...um...detective. What do ye want to know about Brain Bender?"

At that moment, the door opened and Chu walked in, carrying a yellow legal pad. He gave a nod to Jamie and sat in the seat next to Pro.

"This is pretty intimidating," Jamie admitted, looking at the two detectives.

Chu smiled. "Please don't feel uncomfortable, Mr. Tobin. Detective Thompson and I are just interested in anything you might know from your interactions with Brain Bender Press."

Jamie nodded, not knowing what to say.

"First of all, did you approach them, or did they make first contact?"

"Well, I've been working on a book of magic tricks for the last year or so. I knew that most of those don't sell much, because the places where they are published only sell to magicians, which is a small audience."

"That makes sense," Chu agreed.

"So I went a different way. I wanted to write a book that was a combination of the history of magic with me own story, and then had some tricks anyone could do with household objects between the chapters."

"I see," Chu said, trying to sound sage.

"So I sent out me first few chapters to some people I know, and that's when I got contacted by Brain Bender."

"When was this?" Chu asked, his pen poised over the pad.

"About six months ago," Jamie explained.

"And who did you meet with?"

"His name was Mr. Kelley. He was an editor with the UK office. We met in Waterford."

"Waterford?" Pro repeated.

"Aye, it's south of Dublin. They have an office there. Wee little place, just a couple of rooms."

"What was the date of that meeting?" Chu asked. Jamie told him then Chu went on, "What did they tell you at the meeting?"

"He said the publisher liked me writing and wondered if I could focus on just the street performing angle."

"Is there a reason they wanted that change in direction?" Pro asked.

"Mr. Kelly said it would have the broadest appeal. Street Magic is very popular, and it would give me a chance to interview magicians who started out as buskers and add me own story to it."

"And they were willing to pay you to do this?" Chu wondered.

"Aye. I thought it was me dream job," Jamie said, and gave a shy glance to Pro. "It was also a chance to come back to America, maybe see some people."

Pro looked down at the desk, a slight flush on her cheeks.

Damn, she thought, *why does he always make me feel like a school girl with her first crush?*

"Were there any stipulations on this travel, any requests they made?" Chu huffed with an air that suggested this interview was going nowhere.

"Aye, Mr. Kelly said since I would be in New York, they wanted me to make sure their shipments from China and South America got to their New York office."

Both Chu and Pro's heads snapped up.

"What was that?" Chu demanded.

"Kelly said it was a part-time thing while I was doing me research." Jamie shrugged. "It's been barely an inconvenience."

"What do you have to do?" Pro pressed.

"I go to this place in downtown Manhattan. They're a customs brokerage, Transport Logistics. I have to check the paperwork and sign off on it, and then they ship the boxes of books directly to the New York warehouse in Brooklyn."

"Didn't it strike you as odd they would want you to do this?" Chu challenged.

"Mr. Kelly told me that, although Brain Bender has got a big office in South America, its New York offices are a bit small, and they have to keep the staff minimal. I figured since they were payin' me to travel and puttin' me up it wasn't all that much to ask."

Chu rose unexpectedly. "Mr. Tobin, can we ask you to wait here a few minutes while I speak with my partner?"

"Um...sure."

Chu gave Pro a nod and they stepped into the hall and shut the door.

"Are you thinking what I'm thinking?" Chu said.

Pro nodded. "Brain Bender is getting Jamie to sign the paperwork in case anything goes wrong."

"Right," Chu agreed. "They set him up as the company representative so, in case any of the drugs are discovered, they can blame him."

"What should we do?" Pro asked.

"We need to bring in the Drug Enforcement Agency," Chu insisted.

"The Feds?" Pro questioned.

"Yes." Chu thrust the yellow pad into Pro's hands. "You go in there, get any address he knows—the brokerage house, the offices for Brain Bender, where he's staying, everything."

With that, Chu turned and headed back toward the bullpen.

Great, all alone with my ex-lover, Pro thought. *Oh well, my head hurts too much for me to have any interest in sex right now.*

Pro sighed, composed herself, and went back into the interview room.

Jamie smiled up at her. "Just the two of us, then?"

Pro felt her face flush again, but set her mouth in a hard line and gave Jamie a disapproving scowl.

"You look tired, Pro," he said, still smiling.

"I didn't sleep well," she snarled as she sat and tried to make her scowl more intimidating.

"Not my fault, I hope," he sympathized.

Pro's face felt hot, and she was sure that, due to her light caramel-colored skin tone, Jamie could see she was much redder than normal.

She felt her temper rise and spoke in a harsh whisper, "Of course it's your fault. You've turned my life upside down ever since I saw you."

"I didn't mean to—"

"No, guys like you 'never mean to,'" she fumed. "You just show up all charm and sexy, then take off after you've gotten what you want."

He brightened. "You think I'm sexy?"

She stared at him open-mouthed. "Really? That's what you took from that? Damn, I wish I'd never met you."

This gave Jamie pause. "Pro, I—"

She pushed the yellow pad in front of him. "I want you to fill out the address for this shipping brokerage office, the address you're currently staying, and any and all offices of Brain Bender Press you've been to, here and in Ireland or anywhere else."

He looked at the pad and raised his eyes to hers. "I still care about you, Pro."

"Going downhill from the 'I love you' the other night. You only care about yourself, Jamie. Now, write. I'm getting more coffee."

She got up and stormed out of the interview room, making sure to slam the door as she went through. She leaned against the jamb to calm herself down. A part of her wanted to rush back in and slam his pretty boy face against the table repeatedly. The other part of her wanted to go in and rip off his clothes.

So much for lack of sexual interest.

She headed to the break room, where bad cop coffee would be available, trying to master the mix of emotions she felt.

And what about Luther?

She sighed. Luther was not getting in touch, and she was trying to decide if she should try to text or call him again. But to what end? If he had decided they were broken up, she should move on.

This idea gave her a strange sense of loss. Could the problem be that she was the one who had neglected the relationship and not Luther? Could her fear of being the first to say "I love you" have ruined the relationship? Could her mixed desires for Jamie be about not facing her own fear of failure?

She got a cup of coffee and began to head back to the bullpen with the opinion that Jamie should write stuff and stew for a few minutes.

Coming out of the locker room was Julie Barker. She was just coming on duty and was in uniform, but her eyes were red and her face blotchy.

"Julie?" Pro said, concerned.

Julie looked at her, the face of abject misery. "Hello, detective," she sniffed.

She stepped in front of Julie. "Are you all right?"

Julie looked at the floor and tears began to fall. Pro saw that the second interview room across from where Jamie sat was empty. She pulled Julie into the room. "What's up?"

"T-Tom broke up with me," Julie sobbed, and her hands went to her face as her reserves gave way.

Fortunately, as interview rooms were often used to speak to people who had been the victims of crime, they were fully stocked with tissues. Pro pulled a couple from a box and handed them to Julie, who took them, daubed her eyes, and blew her nose.

"I have to go on duty. Bailey is waiting for me," she sniffled.

"You can take a moment to tell me what happened, and maybe follow me when I go kick Tom's ass," Pro growled.

"It's not his fault; it's his parents. They want him to marry a Korean girl. They've been fixing him up with one."

Pro blew out her breath in exasperation. "So what did he say?"

"He told me he should at least try to date her, to see if his parents were right," she mumbled. "And now I have to go on duty and I don't know what to do."

"You'll be fine; you're a professional," Pro said, and grabbed some more tissues from the box. "But maybe take some tissues."

"Pro, I love him," she bawled in abject misery.

Pro took her by the shoulders. "You don't think about it, and focus on being the best cop you can be. You do the job."

Julie nodded, getting control of herself. "You're a good friend, Pro."

She looked down at her shorter associate. "I'm kinda going through the same thing myself, right now."

"What? Not you and Luther!"

"Afraid so. Maybe we should meet up after work and we can commiserate."

"That's a good idea. I've got your number." She glanced at her watch. "Gotta go."

They exited the interview room, and Pro stood in the hall as she tried to figure out why every man she knew did not have a clue.

12. Assistant's Revenge

Pro crossed the hall into the first interview room to see if Jamie had finished writing out the names and addresses.

She went in the door and he looked up at her and smiled.

The desire to do violence went through her mind again. Tom was breaking up with Julie. It turned out her mentor and partner was just another man who used the women in his life.

Just like Jamie!

She sat across from him and glared daggers.

"You look a wee bit angry, Pro," he said as he finished writing.

"Angry? Yes, I am a 'wee bit' angry. Guys like you show up out of the blue and make women all confused. And as soon as you get a deal or your 'big break' you'll be off again."

She slammed her palm on the table and the loud noise made Jamie jump.

"I never meant to—"

"No, you guys never mean to do anything," she railed. "That's the problem. You get stupid women to fall in love with you and then you take off!"

The smile returned. "Are you saying you're in love with me, Pro?"

Pro pushed back the urge to slap him. "No, I'm saying I *was* in love with you. But you took care of that, didn't you?" She stood and grabbed the notebook. "I'll take this to my partner."

"Am I free to go now, Pro?"

"You keep your ass in that chair until I get back."

"But...um...detective," Jamie confessed. "I need to use the bathroom."

She felt a desire to tell him to just wet himself, but she controlled it. "Fine, use the bathroom. It's just down the hall. But I want you in here when I get back."

"Of course, detective."

She stormed out of the room and into the bullpen. She approached her partner's desk and handed him the yellow pad.

Tom glanced up at her as she glared at him. "What's wrong?"

"I ran into Julie," she said in low tones.

"Ah, I guess she told you," Tom sighed.

"I told her to stick around and she could see me kick your ass."

"Could you kick my ass after work? I'm expecting a call back from the DEA."

She leaned closer to him, so that no one else in the room could hear. "See if they can locate a spine for you when you talk to them."

Tom looked around the busy bullpen where other detectives were going over cases and talking tactics with their own partners. "We'll talk about it when we're alone, okay?"

"I'm disappointed in you," Pro said and stood up as she raised her voice. "Should I release the witness?"

"No," Tom said and glanced over what Jamie had written on the legal pad. "The DEA will want to question him. Get him water or something, and keep him here."

"Got it," Pro said as she moved out of the bullpen and back toward the interview room.

And ran headlong into her father.

"Hey, Pro!" Max said as she almost walked into him.

Pro exhaled heavily. "You are the last thing I need today, Max!"

"I had to see you. I found out about that guy from last night, Edward Mandel? He works at Brain Bender Press! That's the name that was on the spine of the books at May Johnson's apartment that were hollowed out."

"We know, Max," Pro scoffed.

"You do?" Max said, a bit deflated.

"Yes, Max, we're detectives, and we're doing our job," she snapped.

"But, I also found out—"

"Save it, Max. We are running this case, not you!"

"Wow, you're in a mood!" Max challenged. "What got you so riled up?"

Pro wanted to scream at Max, tell him off—him and every other man she'd known. Her stupid lover at the academy, Julius Trent, who lost interest when they were assigned to different precincts. Jamie, who ran back to Ireland due to his expired visa. And Luther, who ran off like a coward because he'd seen her eating banana pudding with another man.

And now, the one man she could depend on, her partner Tom Chu, who had always helped and taught her. He was breaking up with sweet Julie Barker, when she thought he was going to propose. He was no better than the others.

"Because every man I know is a coward," Pro raged with a fury so intense it surprised her. "And you were the first!"

"What do you mean?" Max said, taken aback.

"You ran off to Vegas when you had a wife and child, both of which loved you."

Max looked stricken and actually fell back a step. His face seemed to crumple, and his eyes looked wet. "Pro...I...I..."

"Save it, old man," Pro hissed and turned to go into the interview room where Jamie still sat.

Jamie looked up. "Was that yer father in the hall? I've always wanted to meet him."

Pro looked at Jamie, who was as excited as a kid at the prospect of meeting a superhero.

"We're getting the Drug Enforcement Agency down here to speak with you," Pro stated, finding that her anger had dissipated. She glanced through the venetian blinds and into the hall. There, her father hung his head and walked dejectedly toward the stairs.

Suddenly, guilt stabbed at her. She and her father had made so much headway over the last six months, and she'd just ripped his heart out because she was mad.

"Excuse me," Pro said to Jamie and went into the hall. She took several steps and called out, "Max?"

The old magician didn't look up, but started down the stairs.

She gave an exasperated sigh and called out "Dad?"

He stopped and turned sad eyes to her.

"Don't do the puppy dog eyes," she warned as she approached him.

"What should I do?" Max lamented, seeming unsure of himself.

Pro relaxed her shoulders. "You should come up and tell us what you found out."

A small smile appeared on his face. "You called me Dad."

"Don't make me regret it," she muttered, but then she found that she smiled as well.

As they moved down the hall, both of them started to chuckle.

She paused in front of the interview room. "By the way, there is someone who is dying to meet you. He's an Irish magician."

"That young man you used to date?"

"How do you—?" Pro attempted, but then realized the answer. "Mom told you."

"We live together. We talk."

"About me?"

Max shrugged. "We both are invested in your happiness."

"Go in, talk magic. We're getting the DEA here, and then we'll listen to anything else you learned."

"Okay, pumpkin," Max said as he opened the door to the interview room.

"Pumpkin?" Jamie repeated, a laugh coming to his lips, but when he took one look at Max it died. He rose from his seat. "Oh me goodness. You *are* him! You're bloody Max Marvell."

"Was there any doubt?" Max shrugged.

"I dunno, a part of me always thought that Pro was pullin' me leg. But, here ye are!"

"I'll let you know when Tom and I can join you," Pro said, and with a glance that told Jamie, "You're a dead man if you ever call me 'pumpkin,'" she went out of the room.

"Is she always like that?" Jamie asked as Pro stepped out.

"You don't want to know," Max smirked.

Pro returned to her desk, drained of her anger and her energy. At least her headache was gone. She cleared her throat to get Tom's attention. "Any luck with the DEA?"

Tom nodded. "Yes. I was given to an agent who seems to be aware of something wrong with Brain Bender. He should be here within the hour. I am going to go talk to the captain and the LT."

"Good idea," Pro said. "If this ends up being big, we need everyone up to speed."

"But there still are a lot of questions," Tom said, getting up from his desk.

"Max is here. He found the same information about Mandel that we did, but he said he has more. He's keeping an eye on Jamie."

Tom smiled smugly. "Who's keeping an eye on *him*?"

As Tom walked out, Pro focused on her screen as she went over the case reports. She compared notes of the people in the apartments closest to the two victims, looking for something, anything to pop.

Whoever the killer was, he certainly couldn't kill two people, one with a knife and one by breaking her neck, without leaving more evidence than they found. And yet there were no bloody footprints, no fingerprints in either location other than people expected to be there.

The hollowed-out books were just that, empty, and only the one book had the drugs, and they were the same as the ones in the medicine cabinet, which may have been overlooked or even planted there to sell the overdose theory.

DEA would want to visit the scene, and it would do Pro good to walk through it another time. She had to try to piece together how the assailant came into the room and how he left, although she was sure the windows had something to do with either the entrance or exit. Also, what technique could the knife-wielding killer use that wouldn't get blood on his own clothes?

She pulled up the ME report and the autopsy.

"Nice light reading," Max said from her shoulder, which made Pro jump.

"One time, you're going to do that, and I'm going to hit you without meaning to."

"Sorry, Pro," Max said.

"Is Jamie all right? I thought you were going to keep him busy."

Max sat in the chair next to her desk usually reserved for a guest or a victim reporting a crime. "I *am* keeping him busy. I let him try on a pair of my handcuffs."

Pro sat up and looked at Max with suspicion. "You put him in handcuffs?"

"He told me that he always wanted to learn the escape."

"And you happen to have a pair of handcuffs?"

"Doesn't everyone?" Max shrugged.

"Do you think he can do it?"

"We'll see. I gave him a paperclip." Max smirked. "So did the Medical Examiner speculate about how the knife wound was inflicted?"

"You have to stop reading over my shoulder, Max," Pro chided. "But he did say there wasn't any sign of hesitation wounds."

"So whoever did it, knew what they were doing," Max pondered, as she closed the report. "You needn't have bothered. I've already memorized it."

"And your conclusion?"

"That Thomas James' killer attacked from behind, to avoid being drenched in blood."

Pro nodded. "As you saw from the medical report, James' throat was slashed. He was found in the living room with his back to the bedroom. There was a lot of arterial blood spread around the living room, yet no bloody footprints near the door or into the hall."

"You think the killer did the deed with James in the bedroom doorway?"

"Since none of the other residents saw anyone in the hall, or heard James' door open—"

"Then the killer went in and out through the trick window."

"The only reason police were called was because Thomas James had a chance to scream before he went down."

"Could he have known what was coming?"

"I think he may have known he was targeted. I still don't know why."

Max tapped his chin. "Both he and May Johnson had a lot of the hollowed-out books in their possession. At the book club, the members had to turn in their books before they got the new ones."

Pro frowned. "Could they have been switching them?"

Max's eyebrows rose. "Switching them? You mean buying new ones, like I did with *The Muse* book?"

"Right! And then she turns in an ungimmicked book and keeps the one that was hollowed out." Pro stared at the computer screen, which only showed the list of reports. "But why?"

"Collecting evidence, maybe?"

"For what? We know how she may have got the drugs, but who did she distribute them to? We are missing the next people in the chain."

"Shall we see how your old boyfriend is doing?" Max asked with a twinkle in his eye.

"It might be best to not have him locked up when the DEA gets here. They might think we did it."

They both rose and walked down the hall to peek in the interview room. Through the venetian blinds they could see Jamie in the chair. He had the paper clip in his hand and somehow had bent the end of it and was jamming it in the keyhole of the cuff with little effect.

"So are you seeing him again?"

Pro sighed. "He came in to help with the case. Turns out he has been picking up book shipments for Brain Bender."

"What?" Max said, surprised.

"Nice when I know something you don't," Pro sneered.

"It has to happen occasionally, Pro," Max huffed and looked in the window again. "So, are you seeing him again?"

"Luther saw us talking and took off."

Max frowned. "Really? I must admit, I expected more from him. He always seemed very stable."

"Until now, he always has been," Pro sighed.

"Does stable come across to you as 'boring?'"

"It never did with Joe and Mom. I always thought I could depend on Luther. But then Jamie shows up and I'm all...confused."

"The dashing young magician instead of the steady security officer? I can understand that. I married several women who were exciting in the moment. But

I have to admit, these last six months back with your mother have been the happiest in my life."

"So you're saying that maybe 'stable' and 'boring' isn't so bad?"

Max smiled. "Not bad at all. Shall we let the poor young man free?"

They stepped into the room and Jamie raised his head. He held up his chained wrists and asked, "Okay, what am I missing?"

Max gave an evil grin, walked over, and grabbed the bent wire. "You're missing the necessary amount of practice, young man."

He pushed the bent wire into the first cuff and it fell open, then he used it on the second one. Jamie was free and Max was slipping the handcuffs into his pocket.

Jamie looked at his wrists. "That's seriously not possible."

"Of course it's possible," Max scoffed. "But you have to be willing to lock yourself in them and get out, hour after hour, every day, until you can release yourself with your eyes closed. And then you have to study how locks work, how the mechanism functions, until you can glance at a lock and know how to open it."

"I don't know if I'm ready for that," Jamie said.

Max shrugged. "Then stick to card tricks."

The door opened and Tom Chu came in. Pro stiffened, still annoyed at her partner. Behind Tom was a sturdy man in a black suit and horn-rimmed glasses. He had thinning brown hair and looked solid. His eyes went from Pro to Max to Jamie, his mouth a tight line.

"This is Pro Thompson, my partner," Chu said, indicating Pro. "This gentleman is Max Marvell, our civilian lock expert, and the young man seated at the table is Jamie Tobin. He's the witness."

The man, who had an expression like he'd just sucked a lemon, looked everyone over. "I'm Agent Stanton with the Drug Enforcement Agency. I have been assigned to look into the allegations that these two murders may have been related to drug trafficking."

"Let me show you the reports we've compiled," Tom suggested.

"In a moment," Stanton said, his gaze on Jamie. "This is the young man who has been acting as a mule?"

"He's the one signing for the books we believe contain the product," Pro explained.

Stanton pointed a finger at Jamie like a weapon. "He goes nowhere." He then stared up at Max. "You're the lock expert, huh? Detective Chu said you figured out how the killer got into the murder sites."

Max shrugged. "I'm good with locks. Nice pin, by the way."

Pro looked over to see that Stanton had a small gold eagle on his lapel. It seemed to be holding something, but Pro couldn't tell what it was.

Stanton got a smug look on his face. "An expert, huh? Let's just see about that, shall we?" He pulled out a pair of handcuffs, a rather scary looking set. Instead of the flat metal with the small opening, there was a cylinder that rose from the lock with the fitting for a full-sized key.

Max looked at the shackles with admiration. "High-security cuffs?"

"Nothing but," Stanton announced with pride.

"Facing you or behind my back?" Max asked nonchalantly.

"Behind the back, I think."

Max turned around as Pro and Chu exchanged a glance. Stanton put the cuffs on Max's wrists quickly and efficiently.

"You don't mind if I double-lock them?" Stanton challenged.

"I'd expect nothing less," Max agreed.

Stanton took out a small wire with a loop and pressed the end into a tiny hole near the lock cylinder.

"Comfortable?" Stanton asked smugly.

"Quite," Max said as he turned around, his back to the wall. He took a deep breath. "If memory serves me, these are Peerless Model PH702CHS High Security cuffs. I assume you went for the two keys, a different one for each lock?"

Stanton folded his arms as a smile crept onto his face. "I must be honest with you, I've never had a prisoner escape from those."

Max smiled back. "That's because they were prisoners and not performers."

Max brought his hands forward, the open cuffs in his outstretched right hand as Stanton looked dumbfounded.

"How on earth—" Stanton said, unable to finish his sentence.

"Harry Houdini used to do a stage act where he would ask people to bring handcuffs and lock him in them," Max explained. "It was called a 'challenge act,' and he learned enough to get out of any handcuff ever made." He gave a nod to Jamie. "I've always been a fan of Houdini."

Max took the cuffs and put them into Stanton's pocket.

Stanton smiled. "Shall we get down to business?"

"Agreed," Chu said.

Max nodded. "But only if you explain why you didn't want to tell us that May Johnson and Thomas James were both undercover DEA agents."

13. Aztec Lady

Everyone except Max and Stanton stood open-mouthed staring at the magician. Stanton's jaw grew tight as he glared at the detectives, at Jamie, and then at Max.

Stanton spoke first. "Why do you think this, Mr.... was it Marvell?"

Max gave an enigmatic smile. "You mean besides the fact that a DEA agent came down here so quickly when called? Or the fact that you've had people looking into this case ever since it broke?"

"How...?" was all Stanton could muster.

"How about the workers for Zelig Construction that were questioned by your men right after the detectives and I spoke to them? You've had people shadowing us ever since the murders took place."

"Is this true?" Pro demanded.

Stanton gave a look to Jamie. "I prefer not to discuss this in front of the witness."

"There is another interview room across the hall," Chu offered.

Stanton nodded, and the four people crossed the hall. Pro was the last to leave and she pointed at Jamie. "You don't move!"

"Wouldn't dream of it," Jamie reassured.

The detectives, Max, and the DEA agent moved into the room and Pro closed the door.

Stanton looked angry now. "What are you playing at, Mr. Marvell?"

"The question, *Mr.* Stanton," Max said and folded his arms, "is what are *you* playing at?"

Stanton looked flustered and his eyes went from Max to the two detectives.

Max went on. "Two DEA agents are killed and you don't tell the detectives looking into the murders?"

"We could have used that information, Agent Stanton," Chu challenged.

"We were planning to meet with the NYPD soon, but we had to move carefully," Stanton confessed.

"Why?" Pro demanded, and she crossed her arms like her father.

"Allow me," Max said. "Because May Johnson and Thomas James were both deep-cover operatives. Only someone associated with the DEA could know that they were agents."

Stanton's face turned very red and his eyes appeared to bug out at this. "How on earth...? Have you hacked into government files? Because if you breathe a word of this, I will come down on you like a ton of bricks."

Max's mouth curled up at one end. "No need for threats, Agent Stanton. I didn't 'hack' any files or even go anywhere I didn't belong."

"You show up here where you don't belong," Pro muttered.

Max went on. "This was done through a series of deductions based on the evidence at hand. First off, why did they both have books that had been used to ferry drugs? The logical answer, they were compiling evidence or dealing drugs. Since May Johnson's neighbor, Ms. Irving, did not see people coming to pick up the drugs at all hours, I decided it was the latter."

"When did you speak to Ms. Irving?" Pro asked.

"What do you think I was doing after you and Detective Chu wouldn't let me ride with you? I went to the apartment and spoke with Ms. Irving."

Chu leaned to Pro and whispered, "We have to get him a babysitter."

"Or stick him in day care," Pro murmured back.

Max went on, reveling in being the center of attention. "Then there was the construction work that was done to gimmick the windows. That was under orders of the Drug Enforcement Agency."

"How could you possibly—" Stanton bellowed, getting even more red-faced.

"I spoke with the workers, and they had seen a man looking like a *Federale* come by the office to talk to Mr. Zelig the day before the work began on the two windows." Max looked over at Pro. "That's why Zelig's office is closed; the Feds have him shut down."

"All right," Stanton exploded. "I am not interested in your 'deductions' and 'theories,' Marvell. The truth is that you've stumbled across a big case, and we've been trying to get to the bottom of it for years."

"Agent Stanton," Chu said in his calm voice, "we need to know what's going on. We're investigating two murders. Don't you think knowing more would help us find the killer?"

"Do you want to tell them or shall I?" Max smirked.

Stanton's eyes narrowed. "Tell them what?"

Max shrugged and turned to Pro and Chu. "There's an informant in the DEA that is helping the Brain Bender people."

Stanton made a choking noise and sputtered several incoherent words.

"Is this true?" Pro chided.

Stanton got a grip on himself and moved his hand to loosen his tie. "Do I have your word that none of you will say anything to anyone?"

Max leaned to Pro. "That means it's true."

"Yes, we have a leak," Stanton said, keeping his voice low, despite the anger aflame in his eyes. "But if anyone were to know that—"

"Relax, Agent Stanton," Chu reassured. "We've all been there. If this info got out, the dealers would shut down and set up operations somewhere else."

"And you'd never catch your leaker," Pro pointed out.

"Exactly," Stanton grunted as he looked Max up and down. "Don't suppose you know who the leaker is?"

Max shrugged. "I'm only on the case part-time."

"So what *can* you tell us?" Pro insisted.

Stanton moved to the venetian blinds at the windows and peeked out, making sure no one was nearby. He then returned to the others, and they all sat at the table, Max sitting last.

"We are sure that Brain Bender Press is a front for a major drug ring, based in South America and China. Their major product is Fentanyl, and I don't have to tell you how dangerous that is."

"It's colorless, odorless, and tasteless," Pro agreed. "It's very easy to overdose on it."

Stanton nodded. "Especially since the stuff that's been coming in isn't consistent. These fake OxyContin pills that have shown up? The dosage varies from pill to pill."

"Not to mention the crap that is used to *make* them into pills," Chu added.

Pro nodded. "Everything from ash to chalk. If the drug doesn't kill you, what they make it out of will."

Max spoke up. "So, I have to ask, why the trick windows?"

"We needed a way to get May to meet her handler. It was risky, because May was considered one of the dealers and she was never sure when she might be watched."

"So, Thomas James acted as her handler, I take it," Max interjected.

"Correct," Stanton went on. "The trick window was so that in an emergency, May could get into Thomas' apartment, and vice-versa."

"Since the window was a recent change," Max noted, "they must have felt threatened."

Stanton sighed. "They were getting close, and they knew it. But Mandel and Byrne were also getting very suspicious about both of them."

"Why?" Chu asked.

"It appeared that they were moving a lot of product, but they actually were giving it to us, and we were giving them money out of a fund. We think that the lack of actual drug deals is what caused Mandel to become concerned."

"I would imagine so." Max leaned back in his chair. "Think about it, you give out a certain number of fake books, and you get more real books in return."

"Plus, you have to understand, this was a year-long investigation," Stanton pointed out. "We had to get May and Thomas involved in the book club, make them part of the team, and it was a difficult process."

"Does this put you back to square one?" Pro asked.

Stanton pushed his lips out. "It definitely sets us back. But we might be able to use this mule who turned himself in."

"That 'mule' currently has no idea what he's gotten himself into," Pro admitted, her eyes on the table.

"Do any of you know him?" Stanton asked.

Pro lifted one hand. "He's actually an old boyfriend. I think he'd be willing to help."

Stanton set his jaw. "Then the next step is to talk to him."

* * *

"So, you want me to help you catch the people who offered me a book deal, flew me over here, and are paying for me apartment?" Jamie worried.

The others were there, but they had let Stanton do the talking. He had gone over the basics of a rough plan, how Jamie could try to get himself more involved in the operations of Brain Bender Press.

"Jamie," Pro said, "they are paying for everything with drug money."

"And, young man, you're going to have to face it," Stanton told him. "It's not that they think you're a talented writer; they just want a big book so they can stash drugs in it."

Jamie looked down at the table and hung his head. "I thought I had really gotten a good deal for once in me life."

Pro felt bad for him, but she knew he was the only connection they had to Brain Bender at this point.

"Now, who was your contact here in the States?" Stanton asked.

"It was Mr. Mandel who spoke with me when I first got here. He brought in Ms. Byrne to go over how I would fill out the customs forms for the deliveries."

"Can't he just let us know when the next shipment arrives and have your men check it?" Pro suggested.

Stanton gave her a dirty look. They were in his field of expertise and he didn't appreciate the homicide detective putting in her two cents.

"That would be the first thing we need," Stanton affirmed. "But if you can find excuses to go to the office, see where they keep the books. I can't accept that the book club is the only way they distribute."

"I have a new chapter I wrote," Jamie offered. "I could take it to them to ask if I'm going in the right direction."

"That's good," Stanton approved.

"Can we have him wear a wire or a camera?" Pro asked.

Stanton shook his head. "We tried to get surveillance equipment into the offices, but they have pretty sophisticated detection equipment and sweep the place on a daily basis."

"It helps to be paranoid when you deal in illegal drugs," Chu pointed out.

"Plus, if they do have someone 'in the know' working with them," Max remarked, "they probably are aware of the frequencies the DEA uses on its equipment."

"But I'm worried," Jamie said. "I mean, I'm no federal agent or cop. I need back-up."

Pro shook her head. "What we need is someone who can get into the office and find out where they keep the drugs and how they get them out."

"I thought it went out with the books." Max frowned.

"I can arrange someone from the agency to work with Jamie, maybe try to get hired," Stanton speculated.

"Bad plan," Max put in. "Word would get around your office and alert the leaker."

"You think our security is that lax?" Stanton scoffed.

Max sat up straight and leaned forward in his chair. "No, I think whoever is working with Mandel and Byrne has made sure to be able to get into your deep-cover files. And you can see what happened to Johnson and James."

"How about me?" Pro offered. "Jamie and I have a history. People will just assume we're dating again. I can go with him."

"Won't work," Max said. "There have been DEA agents tracking you."

Stanton considered this. "So far, I've been the one shadowing your investigation. I've sent agents to do follow-up, but I'm the only one who has actually seen your face."

"But I'm sure your agency has seen our police reports and would recognize Pro's name," Chu reported.

"I can call ye 'pumpkin,'" Jamie suggested with a wry smile.

"You know I carry a gun, right?" Pro threatened.

"You will need a cover name, Pro," Chu urged.

"How about Penelope?" Jamie suggested.

"You have a death wish," Pro snapped.

"Your mother and I almost named you Clairvoyant," Max said.

"That's not better," Pro growled.

"Sure it is! We were going to call you 'Claire' for short."

Jamie smiled. "That's not bad."

"Wait," Agent Stanton said. "You're telling me that your lock expert is your *father!*"

"Didn't I mention that?" Pro responded. "But he still got out of your handcuffs, didn't he?"

Stanton had to grudgingly agree.

"So, you want to go by Claire?" Chu queried.

"Claire Martin, I guess," Pro said, which made Max smile, as she was using his real last name.

"If we can send in the pair of you," Stanton suggested, "then you can take a look around, get the lay of the land, how the office is set up."

"That's acceptable," Pro conceded.

"You can't carry your sidearm, and you should wear something a little less formal," Stanton suggested.

Pro looked at Stanton with annoyance. "So if I show cleavage, the bad guys will give up?"

"I wasn't suggesting that," Stanton said.

"But I will," Max said.

"Thanks, Dad," Pro retorted with sarcasm.

Max shrugged. "Pro, I've always told you, it's all about misdirection. And in this case, you want to give anyone you meet something to focus on that isn't your face."

Pro sighed. "So when are we going to do this?"

14. Quick Change

The next day, Pro was walking down the street in Midtown Manhattan toward the offices of Brain Bender Press. Jamie walked beside her and kept looking at her, while Pro stared straight ahead.

Jamie was wearing his usual magician garb: nice slacks, a full-cut shirt and a vest, as well as a leather attaché case that contained the chapter he had written.

Pro was wearing a one-piece black stretch velour tracksuit. However, this particular design was more like a pair of shorts and a short-sleeve top that clung to her every curve. It came with a zipper down the front that could be lowered as needed. Her mother had also given Pro a bra that pushed her assets much higher than gravity should have allowed. She also was wearing more makeup than she usually did, her mother dolling her up. Over one shoulder was a tiny sequin purse that could hold little more than the pair of cellular phones she carried. The heels on her shoes boosted her up another three inches in height.

"Pro," Jamie attempted.

"That's not my name," Pro scolded.

"Sorry, Claire. I meant Claire."

"You make that mistake again, and we might end up dead," Pro cautioned.

"You seem mad at me," Jamie fretted.

Pro sighed as they walked. "I'm not mad at you; I'm mad at me. I'm mad about this stupid outfit that Max and my mother put me in. I'm mad because this bra hurts like you wouldn't believe and that I have goop all over my face. I'm mad at the fact that your presence confuses me. I wanted to be over you."

"You're not over me?" Jamie grinned.

"If you don't want me to smack that smile off your face, you better stop being so pleased with yourself."

"I thought we had to look like we were dating," Jamie speculated.

"So, offer your hand, like a man would."

"I'm scared you might rip it off."

Pro smiled in spite of herself. Jamie reached out his hand, and Pro took it, and then pulled him closer.

"This is nice," Jamie remarked.

"Don't get used to it," Pro sulked.

They went into the building on 44th Street just east of Fifth Avenue and gave their names at the security desk and showed their IDs. Jamie used his passport and Pro used a driver's license in the name of "Claire Martin" that Agent Stanton had been able to create in less than a day.

Sometimes, it helped to have the power of a federal agency.

The security man looked at them and their IDs with a stone-face and gave them paper badges to wear.

Pro and Jamie hastily stuck them to their clothing and took the elevator as they were instructed.

On the ride up to the correct floor, Jamie said, "A lot of security."

"I imagine so," Pro said in a bubbly voice that she somehow made work. "There must be a lot of important people here!"

Jamie nodded and was silent, realizing that Pro was now lost in her role.

As the elevator slowed and the door opened, Pro grabbed Jamie's hand and smiled at him as if she were a star-struck teenager. Jamie knew it was fake, but had to admit he liked her looking at him that way.

They stepped into the hallway, and then walked down the hall to the correct door. The company name was neatly printed on the glass:

Brain Bender Press
Publishers of Unique Books

As they went inside, an older woman was at a desk. Pro recognized her, and for a moment she was worried that it was someone she knew. But it only took a moment for her to be aware that the woman was a person she'd seen on camera when Max visited the book club.

"Jamie Tobin to see Mr. Mandel or Ms. Byrne," Jamie said politely, his hand firmly in the grip with Pro. Pro just looked around the room with a big smile, like it was just such an amazing thing to be at a publisher's office.

"Of course, Mr. Tobin, just a moment please," the woman said, and Pro pegged her. She had been the woman that Max had taken the book from at the book club. Now she knew why her book contained no drugs. She already worked for Brain Bender.

Jamie led her to a pair of chairs, and they sat still holding hands. Pro smiled at him as if she didn't possess a brain in her head, putting on a great show for the woman who appeared to be the dragon at the doorway for the organization.

It only took a minute or two, but soon Edward Mandel came out of an office down a short hall. Jamie rose, and Pro stood as well, still holding hands.

"There's our hot new writer," Mandel said as he walked in.

Pro was suddenly aware that he was taller than she'd thought. Since her father was six feet four, and he'd worn the miniature camera on his lapel, Mandel appeared to be average height. But he was about six-three and just a shade taller than Pro on her heels.

"G-good to see you again, sir," Jamie stammered. "I hope ye don't mind I brought me girlfriend."

"Not at all, Jamie." Mandel grinned.

"I've never seen a publisher's office before," Pro gushed. "Is this where you print the books?"

Jamie noticed that Mandel's eyes dipped to Pro's exaggerated cleavage. *There goes the misdirection*, he thought.

Mandel chuckled in reaction to Pro's question. "No, young lady. The books are printed in China and South America and then are delivered here. Your boyfriend is writing a book for us."

"I know. I am just soooo excited," Pro trilled and leaned against Jamie.

"Well, let's show you how we organize it, shall we?" Mandel said. "Come with me."

He led them back down the hallway he'd just come from and they walked to the end. There Mandel pulled out a ring of keys, opened a door, and they all stepped into a small room that looked as if it had been designed for storage. There was a copy machine and a self-standing plastic closet that Pro was sure contained cleaning supplies and implements.

However, in the back of the room, taking up the entire wall was a large metal bookcase. Facing the three of them were the spines of hundreds of books. Pro and Jamie looked up at them, amazed.

"Impressive, isn't it," Mandel bragged.

"Wow," Pro shrieked, her voice echoing off the concrete walls. "I didn't know there were so many books!"

"This and more, Miss—?" Mandell said.

Pro smiled as if she were honored that Mandel had paid attention to her. "Martin, Claire Martin," she bubbled and held out her right hand like a princess.

Mandel took the hand and brought it to his lips, giving a small bow. Pro giggled right on cue.

She's like a totally different woman, Jamie thought, impressed by her acting skills.

Pro let go and stepped up to the overlarge bookcase. She leaned over to look at the books in a provocative way that made both men stare at her hind quarters.

Jamie had to force his eyes to look around the room. Pro was only doing it to allow him the chance to take note of everything in the room while Mandel was distracted.

He observed there were a pair of cardboard boxes on the floor near the plastic closet and noted how they still had bills of lading and custom stamps on them. He could see that one came from China, but the other listed "Columbia" as its source.

Pro stood up holding a book about fashion, and Mandel smiled. "Is this any good?"

"You can borrow it if you want," Mandel assured her, and eyed her outfit. "Not that you need to know anything about fashion."

Pro gave the girlish giggle again that surprised Jamie a second time. He had never heard Pro giggle, and certainly not that way. He decided she was giving an Oscar-worthy performance.

"So how did you two meet?" Mandel asked, taking a look to Jamie.

"We met the last time I was in America," Jamie said.

"Yah," Pro added. "And when I found out he was back, we hooked up. I mean, I had a boyfriend, but y'know, Jamie is much more fun."

Jamie glanced at the ground so that Mandel couldn't see his reaction. Her revelation had been a little too close to reality and it made him uncomfortable. He realized they should have gone over their story, so that none of this would surprise him.

When he looked up he saw that Pro was smiling up at Mandel in a way that suggested she found him interesting.

"Y'know, when Jamie said he had a publisher, I thought it would be, like, a stuffy old guy. He didn't tell me you were hot."

This got a chuckle from Mandel. "I don't think it was discussed in meetings. I hope you'll take the book. Consider it my gift."

"That's so nice," Pro gushed and looked over at Jamie. "Isn't that nice, Jamie?"

"Yeah, nice. I brought those pages for ye, Mr. Mandel."

"Hmm," Mandel said and pulled his eyes away from Pro as Jamie took sheets of paper from the leather attaché slung on his shoulder. "Oh, yes, I'll have Elena review them." He took the papers and began to go through them. "How is it going?"

As Mandel looked down at the pages, Jamie saw Pro reach up and lower the top of her tracksuit's zipper, exposing more cleavage.

His mouth went dry. "I...uh...think the book will be ready on the schedule ye gave me."

"That's good, that's good," Mandel said, as his eyes moved back to Pro, then all but jumped out of his head.

"This was so great," Pro blurted, acting completely unaware of the attention her little trick had accomplished. "I hear Jamie has been doing other jobs for you guys."

"Um...yes," Mandel said, forcing his eyes to Pro's face. "He's been kind enough to sign for our shipments." He turned to glance at Jamie. "You have one tomorrow, right, Jamie?"

"Aye, I do," Jamie agreed, finding it hard for him to keep his eyes where they belonged as well.

"Well, I'm like an actress, but I can always use extra work," Pro gushed. "I mean, if you need help."

Edward smiled. "We always have opportunities for well-mannered young ladies." Though as he said "well-mannered," his eyes were firmly on Pro's cleavage.

Pro giggled. "Let me give you my card."

"We might have something in our warehouse," Edward said as she dug into her tiny sequined purse. "You're not afraid of some lifting and sorting, are you?"

"Not at all," Pro said as she extracted one of the specially prepared cards. It had a specific phone number to a flip phone Pro carried for this case. The card had a photo of Pro that her mother had taken that morning. They had hastily printed up the few cards she would need on an ink-jet printer before Pro left her parents' condo.

Mandel looked at the card. "Well, I'll check, see if we can find anything."

"Goody!" Pro yelped, and again Jamie had to control himself as she was so unlike her hard detective persona that it made him want to laugh.

At that moment, Elena Byrne walked in, all smiles, but she took one look at Pro and her gaze went icy.

"Oh, Elena!" Mandel spoke up, and held the pages aloft. "Jamie brought his most recent chapter."

"It seems that's not all he brought," she acknowledged coldly. "And who is your little playmate?"

"Um...this is Claire," Jamie said.

Pro stuck out her hand to shake hands with Elena. "Hi, I'm Claire Martin. Jamie and I are dating."

Elena stared down at the proffered hand like it was a spider or something worse. She finally took it and gave it a quick shake.

"Claire is an actress," Mandel said.

"Is that what they're calling it these days?" Elena spat, with the suggestion that "whore" might be a better title.

"I was hoping I might be able to get some work," Pro said in her "Claire" voice.

Elena sneered. "I am sure there is something Edward can find for you to do. You're the...type...of employee he prefers."

"Thanks," Pro said, completely ignoring the suggestion. She turned to Jamie and cheerily added, "Everyone is so nice here."

She gave his hand a squeeze to suggest it was time to move out.

"Well," Jamie announced, as he took the hint, "I just wanted to drop that off and show Claire your offices. I hope ye don't mind."

"Not at all," Mandel proclaimed as Elena stared daggers at Pro. "Your young lady is always welcome."

"And you're all set to go to Transport Logistics in the morning?" Elena pressed. "It's our delivery for Christmas."

"Gee," Pro said as if she were a bit dim, "it's only September. Why do you, like, need it so early?"

"We have to get product out," Mandel explained, which got him a dirty look from Elena. "We have to get the books to stores all over the country, and no later than the end of November."

"The books require a lot of preparation," Elena added. "Plus, we have to make sure there are no misprints. We need a lot of lead time."

"Wow, who'd have thought there were so many things you have to do to sell books?" Pro confessed.

Elena snickered. "It's not the sort of thing people think about. Those who do a lot of thinking that is."

"Well, we should get goin'," Jamie observed, and took Pro's hand to head toward the elevator.

"It was nice to meet you," Pro said in her "girly voice" as they walked away.

Mandel gave a little wave as they stepped into the hall and headed toward the elevator.

As soon as they were ten feet down the hall, Jamie spoke up, "That was—"

Pro's elbow jammed him in the ribs, and she spoke over him, "Really nice. I mean, I really like your boss. And he's hot."

As they stood in front of the elevator, Jamie got it. Mandel and Byrne were paranoid, and there could have been cameras and microphones in the hall to pick up their conversation.

They got into the elevator, and Jamie now was aware that they could be observed there as well, so he knew not to try any "out-of-character" conversation.

However, he could work being in character to his advantage. They were alone in the elevator, so he turned to Pro and said, "Thank you for coming with me."

He then leaned in for a kiss, and Pro, with the briefest of glances at the camera, pushed her lips to his.

Electricity whipped through Pro's body as the energy from the kiss traveled down from her mouth and shocked all of her nerve-endings to fiery alert. The uncomfortable bra now seemed to cup her breasts like a lover, and the taut cut of the one-piece track suit now rubbed against her lower extremities in provocative ways.

The elevator reached the ground floor and Pro pulled away, her eyes wide, but she fought to stay in character.

"Would you like to see me work?" Jamie said as if nothing had happened. "I think I can get me stuff and we can hit the Wall Street crowd at lunch."

She giggled and held his arm as they headed for nearby Grand Central Station. Once they were a block away from the building, she pulled him around a corner and let him go, as well as all pretenses.

"That was uncalled for," she hissed, as she smacked his arm with the fashion book Mandel had given her. She quickly glanced around to make sure they were alone, but since it was 10:30 on a weekday, no one was nearby.

"I was trying to stay in character." Jamie shrugged, fighting not to allow a smile on his face because he knew that would unleash all of Pro's wrath. "By the way, you can zip up now."

Pro glanced down at her own cleavage and yanked the zipper up to her neck, her face going a bit red.

"You try crap like that and you'll be walking with a limp," Pro threatened.

"You know how I feel about ye, darlin'," Jamie professed. "I think you feel the same way."

"I think we're doing an undercover job, and you are not going to step out of line, got it?" She pointed her finger in his face.

"Got it," he groaned. "So where to?"

"We have to go back to the precinct, as I'm working. And maybe we can't get surveillance on the office, but I am sure we can arrange something for Transport Logistics."

She stormed off and Jamie followed. He probably shouldn't have pulled that stunt, but her desire in that kiss had been real; he could sense it.

15. The Four Burglars

At the precinct, Pro was able to get a quick shower and change into something a little less ridiculous to get back to work on the case.

Stanton had requested a walk-through of the two crime scenes, and Pro wanted to be there to see if she could get any new insights.

She made a point to place in the pockets of her jacket her regular smart phone, as well as the flip phone that was on the business card she'd given to Mandel. It had felt good to get the make-up off her face and to put the harness with her service weapon back on. As "Claire," she had been dressed in less than her usual attire, but going there without her weapon she'd felt downright naked.

But showered and changed in the locker room and back up in the bullpen she felt more relaxed. They didn't have to go undercover until the next day when Jamie would sign for the latest shipment of books for Brain Bender.

In the meantime, Pro, wearing her more traditional black pants suit and white blouse, got back to work going over the medical records and police reports of witness statements.

She couldn't resist the feeling that there was something to this case that she was missing. Some little piece of evidence that would point to the killer. If Brain Bender had hired a professional, who was it? And where did they get them?

She wished she could go over the financial records of the publisher, but that would take a warrant, and then they'd know the NYPD was on to them and they might run.

She wanted to make sure she brought these guys down.

It was early afternoon when both Chu and Pro headed to Thomas James' apartment to meet with Agent Stanton. Much to Pro's surprise, her father was there when they arrived.

"Are you the only one from the DEA, Agent Stanton?" Chu asked as they reached the front of the building where Stanton and Max waited.

"Yes, it's all about containment," Stanton explained. "Until we know where Brain Bender gets its information, I want to keep this to just the four of us."

Max piped up. "Doug thinks that's a good strategy, and I have to agree with him."

"Doug?" Chu repeated.

"Well," Max explained, "Agent Stanton and I have been talking. He's not only knowledgeable about his field, but the techniques used in hiding things."

Stanton smiled. "I didn't know that Max here was Max Marvell from Vegas. I saw his show ten years ago; best magic show ever."

"Now, now, don't flatter me, Doug," Max demurred.

Pro gestured to her father to step aside as her partner buzzed the apartment of the manager.

"What are you doing here, Max?" Pro grumbled as they stepped out of earshot. "Besides worming your way into my case by kissing Stanton's butt."

"Just doing follow-up, pumpkin," Max conceded.

"No, Max, you don't do follow-up," Pro fumed. "You are done. It is now in the hands of the professionals."

"Then I guess you don't want to hear what I learned from the other members of the book club?"

Pro stared at her father. "You met with members of the book club?"

Max gave his enigmatic smile. "Not only that, I can tell you who the drug dealers are in the group."

"Did you mention this to Agent Stanton?"

"No, honey. This is your case, remember?" Max insisted.

"Officially, we are working with the DEA," Pro asserted.

Max lifted one eyebrow. "Are you now?"

"What is that supposed to mean?"

"Nothing," Max dismissed. "Let's go inside, see if we can find anything."

"I don't recall inviting you."

"If you want to know the book club members who have the drugs, you'll let me in."

Pro's jaw got tight. "That's blackmail."

"Pro, I can help. Won't you let me?" Max offered. "By the way, did that outfit get Mandel's attention this morning?"

Pro stared at the ground. "It got Jamie's attention, too."

"I can understand that. You looked great in it."

"Max, I don't want Jamie's attention. To be honest, I miss Luther."

"You'll have to figure that all out yourself. Come on, let's go inside."

Chu had left the door ajar for Max and Pro, and they headed down the hall to the back of the building. When they arrived in the apartment, Chu was already walking Stanton through the scene, pointing out the kill zone and the escape route he and Pro now thought that the killer used.

Max began to examine the furniture in the living room, as well as the now empty bedroom bookcases.

"Do you need a magnifying glass," Pro whispered, "or maybe a deerstalker hat?"

"Elementary, my dear detective," Max hissed back.

"What's that? The only school you graduated from? Elementary?"

Chu and Stanton were busy going over the individual areas and finally stepped into the bathroom to examine the gimmicked window.

"These are empty bookcases, Max," Pro said to her father. "The books are in evidence."

"So they are, but there is other evidence here."

"Like what?" Pro asked, just before one of her phones rang.

"Better get that," Max said as he prowled around the bookcase.

Pro noted that it was the flip phone for her "Claire" identity. She stepped into the hall and answered with her best bubbly voice. "This is Claire."

"Miss Martin, it's Edward Mandel," came Mandel's big voice through the tinny speaker. "Or should I call you Ms.?"

Pro giggled, like he was the soul of wit. "Either's fine, Mr. Mandel."

"Just call me Edward. I hope you don't mind me calling you."

"No, that's fine," Pro prattled. "I was just at an audition."

"Did you get the part?"

"I don't think so." Pro tried to sound dejected.

"Well, I have a job for you," Mandel said brightly. "I'd like you to be my personal assistant."

"That sounds like fun," Pro exulted.

"Yes, but I'm afraid that this week we are very busy at the warehouse in Brooklyn getting the new shipment in."

"Uh-huh," Pro agreed, not sure where this was going.

"So, I would need you to work there for the next week, maybe two, and then we could move you uptown to my office," he told her, then added huskily, "where you would be under my personal supervision."

Very personal, I'm sure, thought Pro.

Then she spoke, "That's sounds fine, Mr....I mean...Edward."

"I'll text you the address of the warehouse, and I'll need you there by 10:00 AM."

"How should I dress?" She forced a giggle. "I never worked a warehouse before."

"I'd advise work clothes that will protect you: long sleeves and long pants," Mandel coaxed. "But when you come to work for me, you can wear as much or as little as you want."

"Oh, Edward," she breathed. "You're just so bad."

"I have to admit, I am," he chortled. "I'll text you the address. Glad you can be part of our team."

Pro ended the call and strode back to the door, almost knocking Max over as she reentered the apartment.

Her hands went to her hips. "Were you listening in?"

Max shrugged. "You're my daughter. I have an obligation to protect you."

"I can take care of myself, Max," she speculated. "Did you find what you were looking for?"

"Not yet, but I'm close."

Chu moved out of the bedroom. "Max, can you help? I can't seem to trip this latch to open the window."

"It's easier from the outside," Max said as he headed out the apartment door. "I'll be right there."

"How's it going with Stanton?" Pro asked.

Chu shrugged. "No earth-shattering discoveries to add to the case."

"I don't like it that Max is palling around with Stanton."

Chu smirked. "But I think that neither of us is surprised."

"Mandel called. I'm working in the warehouse tomorrow, starting at 10:00."

"Okay then we have to get the surveillance truck and Jamie to Transport Logistics at 9:00."

"That'll work."

"Max also said he can give us the names of the dealers from the book club."

"What? How?"

Pro shrugged. "He said he tracked them down."

Stanton's voice came from the other room. "Detective Chu, Mr. Marvell got the window open."

"Let's go, Pro. After this we can hit May Johnson's place."

Pro sighed. "Maybe then I'll have some idea of what it is we're missing."

* * *

They looked over the gimmicked window at James' apartment, and then the four of them visited the former residence of May Johnson.

Pro had hoped she would get new realizations, but nothing seemed to be coming together for her. A part of her felt she was just too overwhelmed by the case, going undercover, and the distracting feelings she was having for Jamie and Luther.

She certainly was working outside her comfort zone.

When she got back to the precinct and Agent Stanton had departed, she pulled Max into an interview room and demanded he reveal what he knew.

"Well, pumpkin—"

"Don't call me that," she muttered.

"I know that you and Tom were tracking down the people at the meeting, and I just memorized the sign-in sheet the day I was there."

"What sign-in sheet?"

"When I got the paper name tag, I filled out my fake name on the sheet."

Pro had to think for a moment. At the meeting, her father had written out a sticky name badge. The camera had not really been able to get a shot of him doing this, as he didn't lean forward enough for the camera on his lapel to see it.

But with his extraordinary ability to memorize, he had looked at and remembered every name he'd seen.

"Did you write up the names that night?" Pro asked.

This made Max smile. "Yes, I did! Very good, Pro. You know that it is always best to write something up while it is fresh in the mind."

"And you didn't share it with us?" Pro groused.

"I wanted to track them down a bit, see if I could find out more than merely the names."

"So what have you been doing?" Pro asked. "Stalking them?"

"Just some online research, trying to figure out the ones who might have acquired drugs, and who could be distributing them, and how."

"Max, an operation like that would take months and dozens of cops."

"Or just a quick meeting and general observation," Max offered.

"I don't see how you could do—"

"Let's say, I find out about the people, and I do some simple profiling. If they are users, it will show in how they act. If they are merely distributors, there has to be a connection with the users. See how it works?"

"Of course I see how it works," Pro argued. "This is what I do."

"Usually, it is. I have to be honest with you, Pro, you seemed distracted."

Pro sat on the corner of the table and shook her head. "You're right, Max. I'm letting this situation with both Jamie and Luther take up too much of my mind. I mean, we have video of you at the book club, and all the name tags. I should've already tracked down everyone who was there and made a rough assessment."

Max came up behind her and began to rub her shoulders. Pro groaned.

"Hm, I've never rubbed your shoulders when you were wearing a gun."

"I really don't know what to do, Max. When I'm with Jamie, I want to be with him. But when I'm not, I think about Luther."

"Luther shouldn't have run out on you," Max confided and gave her back a pat as he stepped away. "Well, I have to get home to your mother."

"Get this list you've compiled as well as your insights, whatever they are, to Tom by tomorrow."

"I can do that," Max said as he reached into his pocket. "Oh, I want to show you this."

He pulled out a small black box and opened it. In it was a ring made of white gold. The solitaire diamond in the center was a more reasonable size and surrounded in a bezel setting. Tiny diamonds went down the outside of the simple white-gold band.

"The solitaire is less than a carat, but I was told this setting was the best for someone who is always using their hands."

Pro couldn't help but smile. "It's nice, Max, and reasonable. This shows a lot more thought than the other one."

"Really?" Max fretted.

"Really. The other one was trying to impress everybody with a big rock. This one means you're thinking specifically of her."

Max closed the lid and pocketed the box. "I'm going to ask her soon."

Pro gave him a reassuring smile. "You have nothing to worry about."

"Really?" Max hoped.

"She was foolish enough to marry you the first time; she'll probably do it again."

16. Devil's Torture Chamber

The next day, Pro headed out at 8:30 in the surveillance van with Tom, Jamie, and their tactical man, Detective Michael Hayes.

For Pro, it had been another difficult night as her sleep was interrupted with dreams of Jamie and Luther in various stages of undress. Nothing as vivid as when she'd awoken in the peak of a physical release, but she was disturbed by them anyway.

She decided she needed to make a decision and bed one of the two men soon, or she was going to be completely insane from lack of sleep.

She put on a simple outfit that she owned, instead of the sexy stuff her mother had gotten for her first appearance as "Claire." Capri-length pants made of stretch denim that gave her freedom of movement, yet was a pretty sturdy fabric. She topped it with a simple cotton work shirt that matched, and a denim jacket with fake fur around the collar. She was glad she could wear sneakers. The heels she'd worn the other day fit the "temptress" look, but were hardly comfortable or functional. She was also glad she could wear her own bra; the push-up one from her mother was more like a medieval torture device instead of a means of support.

She left her service weapon in her lockbox at home, which pained her. She did pack a small can of pepper spray in her purse. Her real phone and ID would stay at her apartment, but the spray would travel with her, just in case.

At 8:45, Hayes pulled the vehicle into a parking space in lower Manhattan, near the Staten Island Ferry Terminal building in the Battery. They were just outside a five-story building, with huge doors for truck deliveries that contained Transport Logistics.

"All right," Hayes said as he moved into the back of the vehicle. "Do you understand everything about the equipment?"

Jamie nodded nervously. "I hear you in the earpiece, there's a camera on me vest, and a microphone so ye hear everything."

Tom spoke up. "Make sure you lean towards the bill of lading so we can get a good shot of it."

"Aye, I can do that."

Pro cleared her throat. "We'll all be here. But this is easy. Just go in and do what you've done every other time."

Jamie nodded as Hayes checked everything. Finally, Jamie stepped out and headed into the building.

"So today you're at the warehouse," Tom said.

"You're working a warehouse?" Hayes asked. "I noticed you weren't dressed in your usual style."

"It's all part of the case," Pro explained. "I'm hoping to locate the drugs and see where they store them."

"Why aren't you going in with a wire?" Hayes asked.

"Too risky," Chu explained. "Their offices were set up to detect our equipment. We figure the warehouse might be as well."

Hayes turned back to the monitor. "Well, my stuff is working fine now. Your boy is in the office."

Pro and Tom stood behind the seated Hayes and watched the monitor as Jamie approached a desk and spoke to a woman with a pinched face who sat behind it.

In only a few minutes, she had brought out a form and placed it in front of Jamie. Jamie leaned forward so that the page was visible.

"Very good, Jamie," Hayes said into his microphone. "Stay in that position and go through each page, please."

Jamie lifted the pages one at a time, going through each one slowly and making sure it was open long enough.

He then got to the last page and heard Hayes in his earpiece say, "Okay, we got it."

He put his signature on the page and handed it back to the woman.

"My," she said, looking up at the young man, "you took your time with that. Normally, you just glance at the last page and sign it."

"I...um...wanted to be familiar with it, in case they...uh...asked me questions," Jamie stammered.

Then he recalled what Mandel had said the previous day. "It's the new releases for Christmas; it's a big deal."

The woman nodded. "Yeah, we get a lot of that once September rolls around. A lot of people getting orders from overseas that they have to ship all over the country before Thanksgiving."

"Thanks," he said with a wave and headed for the door.

A few minutes later, Jamie was back in the van, and they were removing the camera and the wire. He pulled the earpiece out and put it on the table that Hayes was using.

"How far do we have to take you?" Chu asked Pro.

"The warehouse is just off the Brooklyn Bridge in DUMBO," Pro answered, referring to the area in Brooklyn that was "down under the Manhattan and Brooklyn Bridges." It consisted of many warehouse buildings, and even though some had been converted to living spaces, many were still used for business. "Can you drop me off just off the bridge? I can walk over."

"You ashamed to be seen with us, detective?" Hayes chortled.

"Afraid of being seen coming out of a vehicle that I can't explain," Pro admitted. "We don't know what the security is like at this warehouse. They might have outdoor cameras."

"Okay, Pro, but you make sure to let us know what is going on," Chu insisted.

"I have that number you programmed into my phone," Pro assured. "That will go directly to you, right?"

"Yes, but it will appear on your phone log as a call to Jamie," Chu said.

"Okay, then let's go," Pro said, as Hayes headed back for the driver's seat. "I don't want to be late on my first day."

Hayes moved the vehicle into traffic and took a tunnel that connected them to the FDR going north. He had soon crossed the Brooklyn Bridge, and at the first opportunity, they let Pro out.

Pro walked the blocks quickly. It was easy with her long legs, and the fact that she was in sneakers. She tended to wear black sneakers on the job, and the heels the other day had only slowed her down.

She had checked out the location online the previous night, and the flip phone didn't have a GPS, but she knew where she was going. She strolled down Water Street, where large buildings lined both sides of the street.

Finally, she arrived at the correct address, to a seven-story building with arched windows that had curved brickwork above them. There was a cage of criss-crossing wire in front of each window, and Pro thought that in an emergency, it would be hard to get out.

She took a deep breath and went into the building. There was no security at the door, and she went to the large freight elevator. She pressed the button for the fourth floor, and the huge doors closed as the elevator began to move.

At the correct floor, the elevator opened to face a huge door with a small sign that read "Brain Bender Press." The door was solid and at least ten feet tall. She could see there was a metal roll-down door in a case on the outside, and heavy bolts in the floor where the security door would be locked into position.

Feeling a bit intimidated, Pro opened the door, which required her to really pull as it was quite heavy.

A grizzled Caucasian man with a clipboard was on the other side. He was average height and shorter than Pro. He wore a work shirt with denim overalls and held an unlit cigar in his mouth. He was looking at box after box loaded into a large pile about ten feet from the door.

This main room was huge, and the ceiling had to be at least twenty feet high. It was like a giant fairytale cavern, and Pro noted that a dragon could fit into it easily.

"Who're you?" the man with the clipboard bellowed.

"I'm Claire," she said. "I'm helping out in the warehouse this week."

He looked her up and down as if appraising a thoroughbred. "You don't look like you can handle what we need."

Pro smiled. "I'm pretty strong."

"Oh, you are?" He smirked and pointed to a medium-sized box nearby. "Let's see. Pick that up."

Pro walked up to it, bent and used her knees to easily lift the heavy box. She then returned it to the ground slowly.

"Not bad," the man said. "Maybe you will work out. I'm Joe. I'm the shift supervisor. The rest of the team is in the break room."

He started to walk and Pro fell in beside him. "Yeah, we don't get a lot of girls doing this work. It's a lot of lifting and carrying, and to be honest, most chicks nowadays don't pick up anything heavier than their phones, if you know what I mean."

Pro just nodded. She didn't feel a need to defend herself. Let Joe think she was just some empty-headed broad here to help, and maybe she could find out how the operation worked.

The pair of them stepped into the break room and seven men looked up. They were all different ethnicities. Some were African-American, some Hispanic, a couple of white guys with beards. It was all a blur of faces to Pro.

"Hey, guys, we got an extra pair of hands today," Joe announced. "This is Claire."

She stepped forward to wolf whistles and catcalls from several of the men. She looked at one of the men in the back who had a bald head, just as he looked up.

It was Luther.

The pain in her heart almost knocked her over, as his eyes met hers. She quickly raised one finger to her mouth as if to say, "Sh."

Luther did a slow nod, to let her know he understood.

Joe was regaining control of the men. "Okay, okay. None of that. If any of you clowns say something stupid to Claire you're gonna haveta answer to me."

This made Luther smile. He knew that Pro could probably take any man in the place. He and Pro had worked out together, and she had pinned him the first time she'd tried. Plus, she had those long legs and was a good reach with her equally long arms.

"Okay we got some of the shipment this morning, and we got to finish moving out last week's arrivals," Joe said. He pointed at Luther. "Martin, can you walk Claire through the use of the forklift?"

"Sure, boss," Luther answered with a nod.

Martin? Pro thought as the realization hit her. *Luther is undercover, too.*

A part of her was so amused by this that she wanted to bust out laughing, but she knew that would completely blow both their covers.

But why was he here? And to do what? If he was in an undercover operation, it would explain why he didn't call her and had gone dark. He hadn't left town at all; he was doing a job.

This realization made her heart flutter a bit, and suddenly she felt a desire to hold Luther and apologize for what she'd thought about doing with Jamie.

The team got up and headed out to the warehouse floor, as Pro took a good look at each person, just in case she needed to recognize them again. They were big men, and strong. It occurred to her that one of these large men could be the killer she and her partner had been looking for.

Luther, who was posing as "Martin," approached and spoke quietly. "So, Claire, let me go over how the forklift works."

Luther grabbed a clipboard and led her out of the break room and into the large open space, talking as they went. He was going over the safety features of the machine. Pro nodded as he spoke and found that she enjoyed hearing his deep voice again.

He led them to a section of wall that jutted out to create a separate room. The walls appeared to be reinforced, and a pair of steel double doors were built into the front.

Luther pulled out a strange key that seemed like it was made from a series of connected chains. The individual parts moved as he inserted it into the lock. He then turned the knob and metal supports that went into the floor and the top of the doorway came loose and allowed it to open. The room beyond the doors was not all that large, but there was more than enough space for a full-sized forklift, which currently faced the wall.

"The first rule you got to do is make sure that the doors are open before you start it up. You got that?"

"Seems obvious," Pro answered in her "Claire" voice.

"You'd think so, but the guy I replaced drove right through 'em."

He stepped into the room and pulled one door closed. "Now let's go over the safety features."

Luther pulled the other door closed, and there was less light in the small room now. He moved to Pro and brought his lips to hers.

Pro had been under the impression that it was Jamie's kisses that had made her act so impetuously, making her lose her common sense. She had kissed Luther many times, but it was usually a quick peck, as one or the other of them was on-duty or in public.

Not this kiss.

It was a full-on, open-mouthed, sensual kiss. She felt her tall, strong body melt against his muscular chest. Their lips fit like puzzle pieces that longed to be reunited. It was hot, fiery, passionate, and demanding, and she could feel him growing aroused as he held her. If she could have, she was willing to offer herself to him, right there, right now. He pulled back and she gave a sad little moan as they parted.

He held his index finger to his lips, and she realized that there might be someone listening in on what they were saying.

"Second rule," Luther went on as if nothing had happened, "is that you never raise or lower the tines when the vehicle is in gear."

He moved toward the machine as if he were uncomfortable in his work pants. Pro wanted to laugh, but she just said, "Yes."

He wrote on the clipboard as he went on. "Also never adjust the fork in any way, unless you are in neutral with the parking brake on."

He turned the clipboard to face her. It read: *Listening devices and cameras. No cameras in here.*

"I understand," Pro answered, trying to sound a little bored like she imagined Claire would.

"Never pull yourself into the cab using the steering wheel," he said as he wrote more. Then he pointed at the forklift. "Use the handhold in the front and the back of the seat. Using the wheel wears out the steering."

He turned the clipboard around again: *I've missed you.*

"I didn't know that," Pro attempted to sound bubbly, and took the clipboard, and she wrote: *Undercover. You?*

Luther nodded when he read it. "Always make sure the fork is two to four inches off the ground when you move it. The last thing we need is it scraping all over the floor."

Pro wanted to ask him many things. First and foremost she wanted to know if he desired her at this moment as much as she craved him.

But that would have to wait.

Luther moved to open the doors as Pro pulled the top page and shredded it quietly before slipping it in the trash. In a few short minutes, under "Martin's" supervision, she backed the forklift out and brought it into the center of the room.

Luther talked her through the process of lowering and adjusting the tines so that she could slip the fork into a pallet under a large box of books. She raised the wooden platform and its load into the air, and then with Luther guiding her, moved it to a large metal shelf and placed it there. She then removed the tines without knocking anything off the shelf.

The other workers were busy going through boxes, removing books, and moving them to smaller boxes. A large bunch of the books were stacked on a ground-level shelf and tightly shrink-wrapped in plastic.

Joe watched and nodded as Pro succeeded, but then he walked over. "Okay, okay, but we gotta get the boxes sorted before we store them on the shelves. Shut that thing down and leave it there for now."

Pro turned the key to shut off the forklift and jumped out of the cab to walk over to where Joe and Luther were standing.

Joe frowned. "You ever worked a forklift before, girlie?"

She threw him a smirk. "Who me? I'm just a little girl. I can't drive big machines."

"That's bull," Joe chortled. "You handled that like a pro."

Luther gave her a devilish smile. "That's a good nickname for you."

"I'll stick with Claire," Pro said, annoyed that Luther might have tipped their hand. "Whaddya got, Joe?"

He gave her an admiring smile, then turned to the big box next to him. "You two go through this box. All the books should have the same cover, okay? But some of the books are wrapped in plastic, y'know, sealed. Those you put on that shelf over there."

Joe pointed to the low shelf where the other workers had been placing books all morning.

"What's so special about the sealed books?" Pro asked, trying to do so nonchalantly.

"How the hell should I know?" Joe responded. "Maybe they're signed by the author or something. All I know is that you take the sealed ones, pile 'em up, put them on that shelf, and then we forklift the boxes onto the shelves on the other side of the room. Got it?"

"Yes, sir," Luther and Pro muttered.

Joe walked away shaking his head, as one of the other men came over. He was a big Hispanic fellow with a lot of muscles, and Pro thought she could see some prison tats on his arms.

"How come you get to work with the babe?" the man asked.

"Juan, I'm the one who knows how to drive the forklift," Luther said with a calm smile. "Remember the one time you tried? You almost put it through the wall."

Juan shrugged. "I woulda gotten it." He turned to Pro, his eyes full of lust. "And hey, we're all sorry about whistling at you when you came in."

Pro gave him a wink. "Some girls consider it a compliment."

This made Juan smile and nod. "You're all right," he said as he headed back to the box he was sorting with one of the other men.

Luther stared at Pro, knowing full well that she was most definitely *not* the kind of woman that considered catcalls or whistles appropriate. He'd seen her tackle guys who disrespected her just to prove a point. Her pet peeve with him was that he sometimes called her "girl."

But Luther had to admit, Pro was playing her undercover role to the hilt. He focused on opening the box and sorting the books. The last thing he wanted to do was think about that kiss. It had been weeks since he'd last touched Pro and he wanted her in an entirely new way.

They were stacking books into piles. The ones to go back into the box, the sealed ones that would be moved to the shelf, and any books that were different from the others.

"So," Pro whispered as they went into the box, "have you seen what is in the sealed books?"

"No, not yet," Luther hissed back, and they both came out with books and put them in the correct pile.

As they went in again, she murmured, "You took this as an assignment?"

Luther didn't answer, but nodded as they came out. Then, he glanced up at the ceiling where Pro was sure there were cameras and listening devices.

She went back to work.

17. Bullet Catch

The day was long, the work hard and extremely repetitive. But as the time went by, the sealed books were filling up more than the one shelf.

Pro thought about the sealed books. Could the seal be so good that drug-sniffing dogs could not detect the Fentanyl?

She also found that the sealed books were always in the center of the boxes surrounded on all sides by regular books. Again, this put forth the idea that the boxes could be inspected, but they would only find books. After all, the sealed books looked just like the regular ones.

She needed to get this information to Tom and Agent Stanton. If they could raid this warehouse while the sealed books were there, and those books contained the drugs, they could bring down the whole operation.

She decided that she needed to talk to Luther. If he had been there for over a week, he might have knowledge that would help.

There was a break for lunch, and Pro got a protein bar out of the machine in the break room. She didn't want to risk the sandwiches it held, because they looked as if they'd expired long ago. She also was able to get a piece of paper and a pen, quickly scrawled an address on it, and slipped it into her pocket.

In the afternoon, she drove the forklift, picking up the boxes for all the two-man teams once they were placed on pallets. She moved the pallets onto the large shelving in the room until the warehouse floor was cleared.

By the time 6:00 had rolled around, the men were sweeping up any debris from the space. The big units had the boxes of books stored on them and on the other wall, the shelves containing sealed books were all neatly arranged.

Joe spoke to them. "Good job, guys. Tomorrow we've got all the Christmas books being delivered. We will not only have to separate them, we need to make up boxes that will go to the uptown offices."

A mutter ran through the group.

"Relax, it will only be for the next week. After that we go back to packing up and shipping books out in smaller loads. This big stuff is for the next few days, and we got Claire to help."

Joe looked at Pro. "Claire, great job with the forklift. You gotta knack for it. How about it, guys?" Joe started to clap, and soon all the men were applauding Pro.

They all started to leave, and Pro went up to Luther and held out her hand. "Thank you, Martin, for showing me how to drive the forklift."

His hand met hers and he felt the small piece of paper and took it without reacting. "No thanks needed, Claire. Joe's right, you're a natural."

They parted and Luther left. Pro grabbed her purse and headed for the door. "Hey, Claire," Joe called out. "What are you doing after this week?"

She smiled. "Mr. Mandel wants me to be an assistant in his office."

Joe frowned. "Really?"

"Something wrong?"

Joe moved close and spoke in a low tone. "Just watch yourself. You seem like a nice girl, and Mandel is what we used to call 'a ladies' man.'"

"I'll be careful, Joe," Pro said.

"Okay," the older man worried. "Just so you know."

Pro headed out to Water Street and headed for the address she'd put on the slip of paper that she'd given Luther. It was a coffee cafe she'd found online the night before, and made a note of the location as a place to meet if she needed one. Although it was only a few blocks from the warehouse, she had figured that the men she had seen would either head for their homes or to a bar. A coffee shop after six did not seem like it would be their first choice. Even so, she got her coffee drink and found a booth in the back out of sight.

She quickly took the opportunity to text her partner: *Sealed books at the warehouse. They may contain the drugs. Large number of them. Might be moving them out tonight.*

She sat and found she felt nervous waiting for Luther. Everything she had thought about him since the beginning of this case had now gone out the window.

And then there was that kiss.

She could sense his desire, and it was returned with an intensity that had surprised her. She was afraid that she was just projecting or perhaps it was all in her head because she had so misjudged Luther.

But the moment he passed through the door and stepped into the restaurant, she found her brain stopped arguing. She could watch him, and he moved with an animal grace that was impressive for a man so well-muscled. He was big, strong, and dark—a complete contrast from the pale and lithe Jamie.

He ignored Pro as he got a coffee drink and slowly made his way to the back and out of sight, choosing to sit at a table nearby.

"I'm not contagious," Pro chided. "You can sit closer."

Luther looked straight ahead and didn't make eye contact. "No, I can't. I'm being watched."

Pro frowned. "Are you sure?"

"If I wasn't, I'd be sitting right next to you letting you know how much I missed you."

Pro felt her heart flutter at this thought. "Really?" She sighed, not looking at him either.

"Pro, I owe you an apology. You had dessert with an old boyfriend. I shouldn't have overreacted."

"I tried to explain, but you dropped off the map."

"I know. I had the opportunity to do this assignment, and I took it. What are *you* doing here?"

"The double-murder I caught? They both had hollowed-out books from Brain Bender. Turns out they were both DEA agents. This is where the case led us."

"Is that what this is about? My company was pulled in to investigate. Drugs in hollowed-out books? That might explain why those books are sealed."

"Why was your company brought in?"

"Competitor. A major publisher that doesn't understand how Brain Bender could be doing so well, financially."

"You're doing industrial espionage?" Pro asked, a bit surprised.

Luther nodded. "I even got a chance to look at some of Brain Bender's financial filings."

"I'd love to see those."

"I'll look into what I can do," Luther assured.

With subtlety, she reached under the table and took his hand. "I'm sorry, too. I should have just told you I wanted to talk to Jamie."

"Well, they needed me for this op, and I needed some space to get my head on straight," Luther said and took a glance out the window. "I gotta go."

"I'm working with Agent Stanton with the DEA," Pro told him quickly.

"Stanton?" Luther frowned. "Be careful. I've seen a name like that as a footnote on some payments."

Pro's eyes grew wide, but Luther got up, and with his cardboard cup in his hand, headed for the door.

She watched him leave. She was overwhelmed with a longing for the man, his strong touch, his firm torso.

She drank her coffee and tried to get her racing heart to slow.

She started to watch the vehicles outside and one in particular caught her eye.

Two men were sitting in it, and when she looked at it, she noted that they were watching the door to the coffee shop. Her cop instincts gave her the feeling that they were watching for her.

She considered what Luther had said as he left. That he'd seen a name like Stanton on payments. Could it have been Agent Stanton? If so, that would mean that Brain Bender knew about her.

Questions began to run through Pro's mind: Why would the DEA agent only involve himself? He said there was an informant somewhere in his office, but he brought no backup. What if the other possibility was true? If Stanton was the one being paid by Brain Bender, then he was the informant, and he had every reason to not let Pro and Tom involve more agents from the DEA.

Plus, if he knew she was undercover, which he did, he could have her followed. Would he go so far as to have her eliminated?

Pro rose up slowly and made her way to the counter. She was lucky there currently was no line of people waiting to order coffee.

The cashier, a short woman with chestnut-brown hair, smiled. "Hi! Are you looking to get a refill?"

"No," Pro said, thinking fast. "I just spotted my old boyfriend outside. I have a restraining order, but he found me. Do you have a back door I could go out through?"

She hated using the "damsel in distress" trick, but it was easier than making demands. She also knew that she wasn't carrying her badge as part of the role she was playing.

The young woman grew very serious and whispered, "Yes, come behind the counter and I'll let you out."

Pro went through a small door that the woman opened for her, and the pair went into a dirty back room and to a door that had multiple locks on it.

"Go out into the alley and go left," the woman said. "Should I call the police?"

"No, I'll be fine," Pro told her. "Thank you so much."

She headed out and left, being very careful as she approached the street. Once she had a clear view, she moved easily up the block and pulled out the small flip phone.

She hit the number marked "Jamie" and held it to her ear as she walked and glanced around.

"Hello?" Tom Chu's voice came over the small speaker.

"Tom, I have reasons to suspect Agent Stanton might be dirty."

"What?" he answered. "Are you sure?"

"Is he there now?"

"No, he left a while ago," Tom responded.

"Can you pick me up in Brooklyn? I think they might be moving product tonight."

"Tell me where to meet you."

Pro glanced up at the street sign. "Bridge Street and Plymouth."

"Got it," he said as he ended the call.

Pro moved into the shadows and looked out. There were not a lot of inhabitants milling about, as it was starting to get chilly at night, which discouraged people.

She moved down the block to see if she could peek back on Water Street and see if the men in the car were still there. She reached her hand into the small purse she carried and felt the reassuring can of pepper spray.

She stepped to the corner and peered around, but the car that she'd seen was no longer in the position where it had been. She glanced again and tried to make sure she was looking in the right place.

"Hey, girlie," a voice rasped as a firm grip closed on her left forearm. "You're coming with me."

Pro pulled her can of pepper spray and shot a stream right in the face of the man who'd grabbed her. He yelped and his grip loosened. She locked her elbow and swung her arm over her head, then slammed it down diagonally across her attacker's forearms, which broke his grip. She faced him and threw a throat wedge, hitting him in the soft area under his chin.

The man fell back, now having trouble breathing, as well as the sting from the spray. Pro pulled back and scanned the area, trying to keep moving. She doubted the man would have attacked her alone, and she had seen two men in the car.

Her upper arms were pinned as the second man, who was larger than the first, grabbed her from behind and lifted her into the air. Since Pro was six feet tall, this was not an easy move, and she knew he could not sustain it.

He held her tight but returned her to the ground. Pro bent forward to grab his right leg in her hands and pulled the leg forward between her own legs.

This threw off her attacker's balance, and he released her as he fell over backward. Pro bounced on her toes, grateful she was in the sneakers and not the ridiculous heels from the other day.

The big man started to get up, thinking his superior height and weight would give him the advantage.

Since Pro now knew where her attacker was, she easily moved into position. As he lunged at her, she turned and brought her elbow up into the big man's face. He fell back and Pro moved in close to jab her elbow a second time, right into his solar plexus.

He went down to one knee and Pro showered him with the pepper spray, and he went all the way down in a coughing fit.

Pro moved away from the pair and pulled out the phone to text a new address to her partner.

She knew the best thing was to keep moving, and that if her assailants did pursue, they would do so slowly. She had to admit the element of surprise had worked to her advantage, as well as her training. But, if they attacked a second time, they would be more prepared for her to fight and be harder to take down.

She walked the dark streets as a voice hissed to her out of the shadows, "Pro!"

She got into a fighting stance and raised the can of pepper spray as Max came out of the shadows and into the pool of light from the streetlamp.

"Max?" Pro hesitated, surprised to see her father. "What are you doing here?"

"I thought you might be able to use some help. I have a car nearby. Come on." Max began to head down a side street.

Pro quickly followed. "But how did you find me?"

"That purse your mother loaned you? I put an electronic tracker in it."

"You did what?" Pro snapped.

"I used a lot of radio frequency devices in my show. And I saw that you were in one place most of the day, but then when you started to move I figured I should be nearby."

"The place I was working had devices to detect radio frequencies," Pro said and glanced back to see if anyone was pursuing them. "Maybe that's why they were following me."

"They wouldn't have been able to detect mine. It uses too low a frequency, low power oscillators that transmit about every two seconds and—"

"I don't care, Max," Pro carped. "Where is the car?"

"Right there," Max said as he pointed at a minivan with smoky windows. Pro glared at it but could not see inside, even when Max pressed a key fob and the interior light clicked on.

Max moved to the driver's seat, as Pro got in the passenger side. She didn't know what make or model it was, but her side had enough leg room for her tall frame.

Once in the car, Max hit a button and the lights faded to black. Pro could see out on the street easily.

"Don't worry, no one can look in," Max said.

"How come?"

"Tinted glass, even on the front. It makes it easier for surveillance."

She looked around the roomy interior and noted that there was a pair of seats behind them, but the rear seats were gone, possibly removed or folded into the floor. "Where did you get this?"

"Get it? I own it. I keep this vehicle at the warehouse where I store my equipment. I needed something to move around those big illusions."

Pro shook her head. "Retired, my ass."

"I *am* retired, which gives me the time to come to your rescue."

One side of Pro's mouth twisted up and she exhaled. "I didn't need a rescue. However, I hate to encourage you, but you actually showed up at a good time."

Max glanced in the rearview mirror. "I'm always there for you, pumpkin."

"Don't call me that," Pro hissed, and checked the mirror outside her window to see if either of the men or anyone else was pursuing them.

"You took care of those two guys pretty neatly."

"You saw that?"

"I would have interfered, but it was over before I had a chance to even get close."

Pro shrugged. "They were big, strong, and probably good brawlers, but they aren't used to someone with training."

"Plus, you took them out before they got over the shock that you knew what you were doing."

"I've got to call Tom," Pro said and retrieved the flip phone.

"Why? What's the latest on our case?"

"My case, not yours," Pro said as she called the number up. "Agent Stanton might be dirty."

"Really? How do you know that?"

"Luther has been working the case undercover as well."

Max frowned. "Luther? Our Luther?"

"Again, he would be *my* Luther, as you have nothing to do with it. Anyway, he got a look at their books."

"How did he do that?"

"Max, I didn't get a chance to grill him. He said he saw a name like Stanton in some payments Brain Bender made."

"Oh, really? It was troubling enough when Jamie ended up at the warehouse where you were working."

Pro had not yet hit the button to make the phone call. "Who?"

"Jamie Tobin, of course. I can track him anywhere in the city."

Pro stared at her father in disbelief. "How?"

"When I put him in handcuffs, I slipped a tracker into the pocket of that vest he always wears."

Pro's mouth hung open in disbelief. "You did?"

"I wasn't sure just how much he knew about Brain Bender. I have to say, if he is at that warehouse, it looks very suspicious," Max said as he pulled out his own smart phone. He opened a special app that Pro didn't recognize. "Oh dear."

"What?"

Max held out the screen and it showed a map of the Brooklyn area. Several lights were on it. One was pink, and Pro assumed it was their location and it was the device Max had put in her purse. Two other dots were glowing several blocks from where they were, one blue and one red.

"Isn't this the place you were working today?" Max asked.

Pro looked at the map. "Yes, I think so. What are the dots?"

"The red one is Jamie."

Pro stared straight ahead. Jamie was there at the warehouse? Had he misled her the entire time about his involvement with the drug dealers?

"I'll call Tom and have him get backup," Pro said and returned her attention to her flip phone.

"I think you'll need it," Max replied.

18. Thumb Tip

They drove the van to a location about a block from the warehouse, and Max conveniently had a pair of binoculars. Pro had gotten through to Tom, who was in the midst of calling the 84th Precinct, which was responsible for the section of the city the warehouse was located.

Max had insisted that Pro tell him everything she had done at the warehouse that day. She did, although there wasn't all that much to tell, but she did go through the sorting process and her suspicions about the sealed books.

As they talked, a familiar car had parked near the warehouse, and the two men who had attempted to grab Pro stumbled out and into the front of the building, still wiping their eyes.

"Those are the guys who tried to abduct me," Pro told Max.

"They look the worse for wear."

"They must know that I'm with the police," she groaned. "Great, my cover is blown."

Max stuck out his lips in thought. "That does suggest that you are correct about Stanton. He is the only one outside of me, your partner, and Jamie that knew you were undercover."

"But you said Jamie is in there," Pro said, her eyes wide. "What if *he* told them?"

Max lifted an eyebrow. "That is the other possibility."

Pro's jaw got tight. "We have to go in that building."

"There are cameras out front, Pro." Max shook his head. "They will see us coming. The only way to go into that building at this point is with overwhelming force."

Pro sighed. "Could it be that Jamie is a lot more involved with the drug dealers than he let on?"

"Well, I've only met the lad the one time, but my conclusion would be that they might want to clean up the loose ends. That would be Jamie, you, and maybe Luther."

Pro turned to her father in shock. "Why Luther?"

Max shrugged. "You said Luther told you he was being followed. If they found out that he was also undercover, or that he got those financial records you spoke of, he would be a loose end."

Pro's flip phone rang, and she jumped. Then she opened it. "This is Claire."

"Pro?" Tom's voice said over the small speaker. "I'm near the location."

"We're down the block in a minivan with tinted windows."

"Is that legal?"

"It's Max's. Ask him."

"Max?" Chu wondered, "where did *he* come from?"

"He's been tracking me," Pro explained. "But he's also been tracking Jamie, and he's in the warehouse."

"What is Jamie doing there?"

"Just get over here. There is room for all of us in this van," Pro suggested.

She hung up and looked at her father. "You didn't bring my service weapon, by any chance?"

"I could have gotten it, if you'd asked. You are aware I can get into your apartment, right?"

"More aware than I would prefer."

"I am sure your partner will have a police vest and a sidearm for you."

Pro looked out the window as the unmarked police car she and Tom used pulled up the block. It made its way toward them and parked on the opposite side of the street.

Tom got out and strolled over to the van, slid the side door open, and stepped in, closing it as he got in.

"Sweet ride," Chu told them. "So, this is yours, Max?"

"Yes, indeed," Max smirked.

"I'm surprised it doesn't have gold leaf on the dashboard or something."

"It's my work van," Max dismissed. "There's no one to impress with it, so I went with the regular dashboard."

"Pity," Chu said.

"Do you have a vest and weapon I can use?" Pro pushed.

"In the trunk of the unmarked, Pro," Chu said. "We need to wait for the 84th. They are sending a SWAT team. They are coming in radio silent, but they will phone me when they are about to arrive."

"Why radio silent?" Pro asked.

"Simple," Max told her. "The bad guys are tech-saavy, and they probably are listening in on the police bands."

"Max says Jamie is up there," Pro said, staring straight ahead.

"So you mentioned," Chu responded.

"And possibly Luther," Max added, "but I don't have a tracker on him."

Chu frowned. "Wait. Luther and Jamie are in the warehouse? What are they doing, comparing notes about you?"

"Very funny," Pro groaned.

"Really, detective," Max asserted. "I expected more from you, since you're the senior partner."

"Well, what do you think it is, Max?" Chu grumbled.

"It would appear they knew about Pro being undercover, and that's why they asked her to work the warehouse today. Pretty clever, using a cop to unpack drugs. Then they received the so-called 'Christmas shipment' this morning. If I were them, I would forward that shipment here. Then grab all the books that contain the drugs and leave town."

Chu frowned. "You think they're going to run?"

"Yes," Max theorized. "Tie up the loose ends and leave town. I am sure they already have a plan to move the product. Then tomorrow, they can continue to use this warehouse to ship the legitimate books, if they wish."

"So, the plan would be to remove the 'special' books tonight?" Pro contemplated.

"If they knew the police were getting close, yes. I also have figured out how they get paid using the book club," Max proclaimed.

"Okay, how?" Chu insisted.

"The book club and the new books every meeting. Think about it. They give books with the drugs to certain people. Those distributors sell the drugs and put the cash in the hollowed-out book. The next meeting they give back the book with the cash and get a new book filled with drugs. Now, repeat this set up throughout the country with multiple book clubs, and you can move a lot of product."

Tom's phone rang and he put it to his ear. "Chu." He listened for a moment, and then spoke clearly. "Good. Get into position. My partner and I have to put on our vests." He hung up and turned to the front seats. "Okay, we are going to suit up. You stay here, Max."

"You need me," Max insisted.

"You'll be in the way and it is too risky."

Max folded his arms. "So how are you going to get in if I don't open the door?"

"We'll break it down," Chu responded.

"How about if the elevator is locked?" Max attempted.

"We'll take the stairs," Chu scoffed.

"Wait a minute," Pro said. "I saw the door that the warehouse is locked behind. It would take explosives to get through it."

"What?" Chu worried.

"It was like ten feet tall and reinforced with metal," Pro said.

"See, you need me to pick the lock," Max proposed. "And I could open the front door as well, save your guys the trouble of smashing it down."

"It makes sense, Tom," Pro agreed.

Tom considered it. "Okay, but you follow my orders, got it?"

"Yes, sir, detective," Max announced. "Do I get a gun?"

"Don't push it, Max," Pro chided.

They all stepped out of the minivan and crossed the street, as Max locked the van with his fob. Chu opened the trunk and Pro helped Max into a vest, tightening the straps as she went. Once Max was secure, she pulled a vest over her own head, then took out a handgun from the trunk and shoved the magazine into the grip, pulling back the slide to chamber a round.

"You brought my gloves," Pro said, and pulled out a pair of fingerless leather gloves, putting them on one at a time. She loaded extra magazines into pockets in the vest.

"I tried to think of what you'd need," Chu said. "Are we ready?"

Pro nodded and so did Max. Chu pulled out his phone and sent a quick text. "Move out," he said and slammed the lid of the trunk. The three people headed for the building, and as they drew near, a large panel truck pulled up in front of the entrance and a rear door opened. A dozen Emergency Service Unit officers in full riot gear and helmets stepped out of the vehicle and down onto the street.

They quickly formed a row, each with AR-15s in their hands as a white-haired man moved to meet Chu. He was about six feet tall with a large mustache the same white as his hair.

"Detective Chu?" the man said. "I'm Lieutenant Reynolds. This is my team."

"This is Detective Pro Thompson and Mr. Martin, our consultant who can open any of the locks."

Reynolds frowned. "When did NYPD start using locksmiths?"

Pro spoke up. "The entrance to the space has a huge reinforced door. Mr. Martin can get us through it."

Reynolds lifted one eyebrow. "We'll see. Now, do we smash in that front door, or does your 'expert' open it?"

"On it," Max said, as he moved to the entranceway.

"We might have some hostages up there, lieutenant," Chu said. "We think they are shutting down this operation, and they may have captured the people who know about it."

"You said on the phone this was a drug operation, is that right, detective?" Reynolds asked.

"Yes, sir. Opioids."

"Then let's get in there," Reynold said, and looked over to see Max holding the door open for his men.

Reynolds considered this, then signaled his team to go in. They passed through the door single-file.

"Fourth floor," Chu shouted and joined them.

Max moved to the elevator. "I'll meet you up there." Pro joined him. "Hey, you don't feel like walking either?"

"Someone has to keep an eye on you, Max," Pro disclosed.

Max moved to the buttons on the elevator panel and quickly put two small flat pieces of metal into the opening in the lock next to the fourth floor button. In seconds he turned it and pushed the button, and the elevator door closed and the conveyance began to rise.

It opened to the fourth floor, where the men were outside the large heavy door that separated the warehouse from the rest of the building.

Reynolds was there, and he was breathing heavily from coming up the flights of stairs. He looked at Max and Pro. "Can you get this open?"

"I think so," Max said and moved to the lock.

"Detective," Reynolds inquired of Pro, "you seem familiar with the door. Was there any kind of bar on the inside?"

"I didn't see one, lieutenant," Pro confirmed.

Max stood up with his hand firmly on the door handle, holding it in place. "It's open, sir."

Reynolds looked surprised. "How many locks?"

"Three, sir. I hope they didn't hear me."

Reynolds stepped up and grabbed the door handle as Max stepped away. Two men with large rifles moved forward, and Reynolds said, "I want a pair of flash-bangs in there, before we go in."

Each man pulled a cylinder from one of the pockets of their vest, and each pulled the pin and held the safety lever in place. Reynolds nodded, opened the door a crack, and bellowed, "NYPD! Hands in the air."

The two men threw in the grenades, and the lieutenant shut the door, a moment later, there was a pair of '*whump*' sounds they could hear.

Reynolds yanked the door open again, and the team of men moved into the room, two by two, weapons raised.

Pro gave Max a hard look. "You move from here, and I will bust your ass."

"No problem, Pro," Max said.

Pro and Chu moved to the doorway and into the room. Men were moving about with shouts of "Clear" as the break room was checked.

Numerous new boxes were in the warehouse, which surprised Pro as they had cleared out the old boxes during her working shift. But now there were many new boxes that took up space all over the room, and from her current point of view, she couldn't see any of the shelves that were close to the floor.

"How did they get these new boxes in here?" Pro asked aloud.

Tom spoke up. "Look, Pro, are those the guys who tried to grab you?"

The detectives turned to find that the ESU team had several people on the floor. Pro recognized the two men who had tried to abduct her. But there were also two of the warehouse workers on the floor with the criminals, but no sign of Jamie.

"Lieutenant," Pro yelled out. "Have you found anyone else, maybe a red-haired man?"

"These are the only men we found."

Pro looked over at the small room that housed the forklift, where Pro had kissed Luther a few short hours ago.

Pro went out to the hall and called out to her father. "Max, are you sure Jamie is here?"

Max quickly retrieved his phone, set it to the correct application, and held out the screen. Both her pink light and Jamie's red light were blinking in the same location.

"Then, there can only be one place where he could be," she sighed. "Follow me, Max."

They walked into the room, with the team of officers in body armor and the captured men lying on the floor. One man was placing handcuffs on the prisoners. Pro led him to the door to the forklift enclosure.

Max looked at the lock on the door and frowned.

"What's wrong?" Pro asked.

"This is something different," Max murmured. "Did you see the key?"

Pro thought back to when Luther had opened the door. "Yeah, it was strange; it was like a little chain in the shape of a key."

Max exhaled heavily. "A chain lock. I didn't think they still made those."

Lieutenant Reynolds moved forward. "I could just shoot the lock."

Tom moved next to him. "Might not be safe if anyone is in there."

"There are also metal bars that go into the floor and doorway," Pro worried. "If you shoot the lock, it might jam those in place, and we'll never get the door open."

"Can you handle it, Mister Consultant?" Reynolds jibed.

Max moved close to Pro. "I don't know if I can open it."

Pro smirked. "You mean the great Max Marvell has finally been defeated by a lock?"

Max gave his daughter a dirty look. "I didn't say that."

He sat on the floor and pulled off his right shoe. He then hit a catch, the heel opened up, and Max removed several different tools. The ends of them looked a bit like dental instruments, except that they were all flat pieces of metal.

He took out a small bent, flat metal tool and put one bent end into the lock. He moved it a little and added tension. He followed it with a thin piece of metal shaped with a point at one end, which grew thicker diagonally where he held it. Max began to slowly insert the metal into the keyhole, bending and adjusting the thin metal as it went in.

He muttered under his breath and pushed the little tool up and down in the lock, then turned the keyhole with the other tool, and the lock came open. He twisted the handle and the assembled group could hear the metal bar disengage at the top and bottom of the door.

Max stepped back as he slipped his tools into his pocket, and pulled the double doors open.

Inside the room in two chairs were the tied-up figures of Luther Ardoin and Jamie Tobin. Max, Pro, and Chu leapt forward and pulled at the cords binding them. Max pulled a gag off Luther's face and he spat out a piece of cloth from his mouth.

"We heard you, but we couldn't let you know we were here," Luther said in a dry, cracked voice.

Lieutenant Reynolds pulled a knife from a sheath on his thigh and offered the handle to Max. Max took it and cut away the rope that secured Luther to his chair.

Meanwhile, Pro had pulled the gag off Jamie's face, and he also pushed out a piece of cloth that had been in his mouth, making spitting noises as he did.

"What happened?" Pro asked, as she took the knife from her father and cut Jamie's bonds.

"Two men came to me apartment and told me I had to go wi' them," Jamie explained. "They drove me to this warehouse, brought me up here, and tied me up. About a half hour later, they brought in this other fellow."

"He's right," Luther gasped. "They brought me in, and he was already here."

"Are either of you hurt?" Lieutenant Reynolds barked. "Do you need medical attention?"

Jamie and Luther shook their heads, as each one stood.

"Thanks for the rescue," Jamie said, his eyes on Pro.

But Pro wasn't looking at him. Her eyes were on Luther. She moved to the big man almost in a dream, and her hand went to his face. "Are you sure you're okay?"

He met Pro's eyes and couldn't fight a wide smile. "I am now, Pro."

Max's voice called from the other room. "Lieutenant, detectives, I think you may have a problem."

Pro pulled her eyes away from Luther and glanced to Tom. They moved to the open door and back into the main room. The lieutenant followed them and bellowed, "What is it now?"

Max was standing in the middle of the room, looking around the warehouse. "Pro, didn't you tell me that they had books sealed in plastic?"

Pro couldn't see the shelves where they had put the books as the new boxes blocked her view. "Yes, it's the shelves behind you."

Max turned and pulled one of the big boxes away.

The shelves that had contained the sealed books were empty.

"So where did they go?" Max asked.

19. Elmsly Count

Everyone captured at the warehouse raid was taken away to the 86th Precinct and it took hours. The men who abducted Jamie and Luther refused to speak without a lawyer, and uniformed officers arrived to escort them.

Chu called his own lieutenant, and it was agreed that they had probable cause to raid the Brain Bender offices. Lieutenant Dunton told Chu that they were on it, and that he and Pro should remain in Brooklyn.

It took some searching, but they located another freight elevator in the back of the building, which led to an exit on Plymouth Street.

Pro had not been aware it was even there.

The ESU team and the detectives went through the new boxes, but found no books wrapped in plastic, and the boxes were only half-full.

Finally, Lieutenant Reynolds ordered that Jamie and Luther be released but told them to give an official statement the next day at the Midtown North Precinct with Detectives Chu and Thompson. Uniformed officers were left on the scene and the assault team left, as did Pro, Tom, Max, Luther, and Jamie.

Once out front, Max turned to the group. "Anyone need a ride?"

Jamie raised a hand. "If you're goin' to Manhattan."

"I have to get the unmarked vehicle back," Chu announced. "I'll need your vests and, Pro, give me the gun."

"Thanks for your help, Max," Pro said to her father as she pulled the magazine from the pistol and cleared the chamber.

"Thanks for everything, Pro," Jamie said and gave a wave to the detectives as he got into Max's van.

"I'm escorting you home," Luther said to Pro as the car and van drove off.

She looked at him. "Please do. We can walk from here."

They started heading off toward Pro's apartment. As they walked, she very gently reached out and took his hand.

"I owe you an apology," Pro said. "I should have told you I wanted to talk to Jamie. But it was only to tell him—"

"It doesn't matter at all, Pro," Luther responded seriously. "And I'm the one who owes *you* an apology. I know you better than that and I just jumped to conclusions."

"I guess we both acted foolishly."

"No, Pro, you might have acted foolishly, but I've been acting just plain dumb."

She looked over at Luther. "What do you mean?"

"It didn't hit me until I saw you with Jamie that I could lose you. I've been taking it too laid back."

"I still don't get it."

Luther stopped and turned to face her. "I'm not good at expressing myself, Pro. But I'm in love with you."

Pro's mouth fell open in shock, as her heart felt warm like there was a little fire within it. "I was afraid you didn't feel that way."

"Well, I do, Pro. I love you and I want to be with you. No one else, just you, and I want you to only be with me."

"I...I love you, too," Pro stammered, almost not believing that she was saying it.

He looked at where they were. "That's your apartment across the street, isn't it?"

"Yes," Pro said. "Can you escort me up the stairs?"

"I can do that."

"And into my bed?" she smiled.

"It would be my pleasure."

They walked up the flights of stairs and into Pro's small apartment. She stopped in the bathroom as Luther opened up the sofa bed. Soon, they were in each other's arms and clothing fell away. Luther's hands went to her breasts and caressed them as he murmured, "Don't know why it was so hard to say."

"Doesn't your mouth have something to do that doesn't require talking?" Pro groaned, and he moved his mouth to her breast and it took her breath away, then he kissed her taut belly and moved farther down.

She gasped and moaned, completely ready to take and give pleasure, now convinced she had made the right choice and was with the right man. That knowledge gave her a sense of freedom she'd not felt before.

Sounds of joy were pulled from her throat, and as she lay back and raised her legs, he moved on top of her and into her. She cried out and he let out a moan of his own as they became one. This was what she craved, the closeness, the wanting. She needed him, yearned for him, and had to have him.

Incoherent sounds came out of her again and again as wave after wave rose and crashed against the shore of her inner woman. Feelings unlike any she'd experienced before shuddered through her body until both of them were reduced to nothing but pleasure and desire.

When they finished, both of them panting, they lay together joined as one person. Luther wanted to move off her, but she clung to him, wanting their union to last as long as possible. Finally, as the ardor calmed, he slipped out of her and lay next to her as she touched and caressed his body.

"I love you, Luther," she sighed.

"I love you, Pro," he said and lay back in the bed as sleep pulled at him.

She lay next to him and examined him as he fell asleep. She watched him breathing steadily and felt completely fulfilled. The problems had all been in her head, and once he'd confessed his love, something she held back had broken loose. Freed from her limitations, their lovemaking had been better than at any other time, or anything she'd experienced with anyone else.

Finally, exhaustion pulled her down and she drifted off to sleep lying next to the man she loved.

But one last thought occurred to her as she fell into sleep: *Who cleared out the warehouse and where did the books go?*

* * *

The morning light and her clock alarm greeted Pro far too early. But she rolled over and felt the warm, strong body next to her and hugged him fiercely. She wanted to make love again, to cement their bond, but she knew she had to get ready.

She was out of bed and into the shower before he could wake. Once cleaned, she had to slip past the folded-out bed to get her clothes, and one of Luther's hands reached out to stroke her naked flank.

She slapped it away. "No time," she gasped as she stepped into the large closet.

"You're beautiful," Luther said in a sultry voice.

"I can't. If we do it, then I'll smell of sex all day."

This made Luther smile. "I'm okay with that."

Pro shook her head as she pulled on a bra and panties. "Men are so weird."

"Can we see each other tonight? My place?"

She looked at him, naked in her bed, and couldn't avoid noticing that he'd woken up aroused. How did guys do that?

"If I can. I have no idea what is waiting for me at work. The bad guys got away."

"Not all of them," Luther said. "Look, I can get you a peek at the financials—"

"After last night in Brooklyn, my lieutenant ordered a raid on the offices for Brain Bender," Pro said as she pulled on a blouse, wanting to be fully clothed so she wasn't tempted to jump back into bed and have another go with Luther. "Let's see what they found, first."

He rose out of bed, stark naked, his muscles flexing and his dark skin almost glowing in the subdued light. He turned around, which showed off his tight rear end, and proceeded to make the bed and fold it back into the couch. He put the cushions in their correct place.

Pro smirked. "That's the sexiest thing I've ever seen."

"What, my butt?" Luther wondered as he stood up straight.

"No. A man cleaning up." She moved to him and put her lips to his, feeling his firm nude body against hers.

"Mm," Luther sighed. "I'll bring my duster next time."

Pro glared at her watch. "Damn!" Her hands unbuttoned her blouse and she unhooked her bra.

Luther frowned. "I thought there wasn't enough time—"

"Shut up and sit down," Pro said, as she pushed Luther into the couch and yanked off her panties. "You have work to do."

* * *

Miraculously, she strode into the precinct right on time, though she couldn't stop for a coffee on her way.

Although the bust had not been a success, she was in a very good mood. It was amazing how a little lovemaking improved one's attitude toward life.

She walked into the bullpen to find Tom sitting there looking glum. "Morning, partner."

"Morning," Tom griped. "You look happy."

"Luther and I got reacquainted." Pro beamed as she sat. "Any word on the raid on the Brain Bender offices?"

"They didn't get in there until about three in the morning," Chu told her, not looking away from the computer. "It took that long to assemble the team, and get the permissions from the building manager."

"How did that go?"

"They had cleared out by the time our team went in. A lot of books were still there, but the computers had their hard drives removed and anything of value is gone."

Pro sat in her chair heavily, her mood ruined. "How could the informant with the DEA warn them? It was a police raid."

"I have no idea. But I haven't been able to get Agent Stanton on the phone either."

"Luther said that some payments had been made that had his name in the memo area."

"I know, Pro, you told me that. But if you think he's involved, we need actual proof. The guys that were arrested at the warehouse aren't speaking to the police. Jamie and Luther didn't see anyone but their abductors before they were locked in that forklift room."

Pro's phone made its tone for an incoming message. She pulled it out to see that it was from Max. It read:

Red Hook Terminal
Pier 9A
Noon

As she read it, Tom's phone also signaled an incoming message.

"Your father just texted me," Tom said with a glance at his phone.

"Me, too. Does yours say Red Hook Terminal?"

"Yes. Rather cryptic, isn't it?" Tom mused. "I'd better ask Lieutenant Reynolds with the 84th Precinct to meet us there. I don't need to step on toes."

"I'll file our incident report from last night," Pro said.

They both went to work, and after an hour, Pro decided she had to risk the precinct cop coffee, as she just couldn't wait for a cup any longer. "I'm getting coffee."

Tom nodded. "I'll go with you; I need a break."

They both walked down the hall just as Officer Bailey came in with a man in handcuffs. Right behind was Julie Barker, and she had her nightstick out as they made their way to booking. Her right eye was swollen and red and was beginning to turn purple.

Chu stopped and his mouth fell open at the sight of her.

"Officer," Pro fretted, "what happened to your eye?"

"You got him?" Barker quickly asked her partner, who nodded and kept walking to booking. She looked up at Pro. "Guy grabbed a lady's purse, ran for it. I tackled him and he hit me."

Chu finally got his mouth to work. "Julie, you're hurt."

"It's nothing," Barker said. "But now we're adding assault of a police officer to his rap sheet."

Chu looked at the interview room just down the hall. "Can I speak to you?"

Julie crossed her arms, still holding the nightstick, which made her more intimidating. "I don't think we have anything to discuss, detective."

"Please," Chu said, his head lowered and his eyes pleading.

Julie took a deep breath. "Okay."

The pair walked to the interview room as Pro got her coffee. It was terrible, even with powdered cream and lots of sugar, but she needed it.

She wanted to just return to her desk, but her curiosity got the better of her, and she paused outside the interview room. The blinds were drawn so she couldn't look in, but as she drew near, she heard Julie scream.

Pro grabbed the handle and burst into the room, not sure what to do. She found Julie standing, her mouth open in shock, and directly in front of her was Tom Chu, down on one knee with a jewelry box open. In the box was a diamond ring. The gem in the center was not very big, but Pro knew immediately what it was: an engagement ring.

Chu gave Pro a dirty look. "Bad timing, Pro."

Pro put on a smug smile and closed the door behind her. "Oh, I am *not* missing this."

Tears were streaming down Julie's face and she looked in shock from Tom to Pro and back to Tom again.

Tom looked up at her from his kneeling position nervously, and murmured, "You haven't said yes."

Julie seemed shocked by this, and blurted, "Oh! Yes, yes, Tom, I will marry you."

Tom stood and she all but tackled him to the floor as she grabbed his neck and pulled him into a hug. She took his face and began to kiss him again and again.

"Nice work, partner." Pro smiled and opened the door to return to the bullpen.

A few minutes later, Tom returned to his desk tucking in his shirt and rearranging his hair.

Pro's eyebrows shot up, and she leaned in to ask him in a low voice, "What did you two do in there?"

Tom looked puzzled, and then got the hint. "Nothing, just hugging and a lot of kissing, and me trying to calm her down."

"What changed your mind?" Pro smirked.

"I've been miserable ever since I told her I was seeing the Korean girl."

"It's been, like, three days."

"Felt like forever," Tom muttered. "So, last night, after the bust, I went to my parents and told them that I wanted to marry Julie."

"How did they react?"

"They weren't pleased, but I told them it was the only way I would ever be happy."

"Really? That was all?" Pro questioned.

A small grin appeared on Tom's face. "Well, that... and the fact that my *Oma* really wants to be a grandmother and is tired of waiting."

Pro smiled back. "I think your parents will like Julie."

Tom shook his head. "Doesn't matter, *I* like Julie. In fact, I don't want to be with anyone else." He rose from the desk. "So we have time before this meeting with Max. Shall we do a walk-through at the Brain Bender offices?"

Pro threw her half-full cup of coffee into the wastebasket. "Good plan. I'll buy us both some good coffee."

"I'm sold."

They headed for the door. "I'm proud of you, partner. I think you're doing the right thing with Julie."

"Does that mean you're not going to kick my ass, now?"

They headed out to their unmarked car. "There's always tomorrow."

20. Magic Coloring Book

Pro and Tom spent the next hour at the Brain Bender offices, but there was little to see.

All of the computers had their hard drives erased, and desks had been hurriedly emptied. The paper shredder was filled with very well-destroyed documents.

The only thing that appeared untouched was the storage room. It still contained the shelves full of books.

At 11:55 they arrived at Pier 9A. There was a large ship that was loading metal shipping containers using the seaport's giant crane. Several containers were still on the pier, but the vessel already had dozens of the rectangular steel boxes loaded on its deck.

Lieutenant Reynolds had assembled in the parking lot with his task force, men and women in body armor who carried assault rifles.

As Chu drove up and the detectives exited the vehicle, Reynolds stood and stared at them. It was a clear day and the sun was warming the air, so he was sweating in his armor.

"What's this about, detectives?" Reynolds glowered as Pro and Chu drew near. "You better not be wasting my time."

"We never would, lieutenant," Chu revealed. "But I am afraid we are in the dark about this as much as you are."

This did not please Reynolds. "Then who *does* know what's going on?"

Their attention was drawn to a figure coming out from behind several of the containers and walking down the pier toward them.

It was Max.

Chu leaned a little closer to Pro. "Does he have to do everything with so much drama?"

Pro gritted her teeth. "You're asking me?"

"Lieutenant, detectives, so good of you to come," Max announced as he drew near. Pro could see he had blue latex gloves on his hands. "You brought reinforcements! That might come in handy."

"You'd better explain yourself, Mr. Martin," Reynolds barked.

"I'd be delighted." Max grinned. "I think you can leave the support team here. Just you, lieutenant, and the detectives."

Max turned, and Reynolds gave a dirty look at his back, then followed, as did Pro and Tom.

They arrived at the front of one of the containers, and Max faced them with a look of glee on his face.

"I don't know if Pro mentioned to all of you that I tracked her with a small device of my own creation last night."

"They know, Max. What of it?" Pro demanded.

"What I didn't tell you was that I also put one on Agent Stanton."

Lieutenant Reynolds frowned at this. "Who is Agent Stanton?"

Chu turned to him. "He was our DEA contact."

"Yes, and I have been suspicious of him the entire time, showing up when he did and all," Max said. "So, I put one of my trackers on him as well."

Pro stared at her father in disbelief. "How?"

"Those handcuffs of his? When I put them back in his pocket, I attached the same tracker I used to find you."

Pro's mouth hung open in disbelief. "You did?"

"Yes, and I was very surprised to see that he was at the warehouse and this pier last night."

Pro recalled the previous evening and the screen of Max's phone showing her pink dot, Jamie's red, and another dot that was blue. "Stanton was the blue dot!" she yelped.

Reynolds cleared his throat. "I didn't see a DEA agent there."

"That's because by the time we raided the building, he had already left...with the books that were filled with drugs."

Reynolds folded his arms. "How do you know that?"

"Because, after I left the scene last night, I've been tracking him."

"Max," Pro seethed. "What does that have to do with us coming here?"

"Because, this is where the trail ended for Agent Stanton."

He pointed to the container behind him. It was large and painted a bright yellow, and the door was closed, but a large red metal contraption was lying on the ground.

"What is that?" Pro asked about the device.

"A heavy-duty cargo door lock," Max replied. "It wraps around the bars; much more effective than a padlock."

"So, you did your lock trick again?" Reynolds asked.

"But I think you'll appreciate what I found," Max responded, and lifted a substantial metal lever, which opened the locking bar on the front door. The right leaf of the double door came open and the group looked into the container that accommodated about a dozen or so large cardboard boxes.

The boxes were lined against both walls of the metal structure, leaving a center aisle where anyone could walk. There were cloth belts tightened with ratchets that kept the boxes in position within the container.

One of the boxes' seals was broken, and a book was on top of the closed box. The plastic wrap had been removed, and the book was open to reveal a cut-out space, and it was filled with a good-sized bag of pills.

Pro moved up and looked at the bag. "Do all of these boxes contain—"

"Hollow books filled with drugs," Max interrupted. "Brain Bender received a large shipment yesterday. They rented a truck to move the shipment to the warehouse. But, they sorted the drug-filled books and placed those in this container. Then they went to the warehouse, dropped off the remaining books, and picked up the drug-filled books from there."

"So they consolidated all the drugs here," Pro declared.

"Correct! They knew the police were on to them and were making their escape. This ship will make a stop in Atlanta, which is where I believe they were taking the product—"

"How do you know that?" Chu interjected.

"I've seen the ship's manifest." Max shrugged.

Reynolds frowned. "How the hell did you find this container?"

"That was easy," Max said. He walked the center aisle and slapped the sides of the boxes, until he reached a very large one that made a hollow sound in response. He then pulled out a small box cutter and sliced through the tape on the top and opened the box.

The others approached and looked in, and Pro gasped.

Inside the man-sized box was Agent Stanton. He was tied in place with zip cords around his body and legs. On his wrists were his own pair of high-security handcuffs, and there was tape over his mouth.

"Is he dead?" Tom asked.

"I don't think so, but I am sure he was drugged."

Pro felt the man's neck. "There's a pulse, and it's steady."

"We should get him the hell out of there," Reynolds said.

"We should probably let people with medical training do it, so as not to injure him," Max suggested. "Detective Chu, perhaps you should call the DEA and let them know where their agent is?"

Tom nodded and went outside to make the call.

"Look, if you knew this man was here, it was irresponsible of you to just—"

"I think Agent Stanton got no less than he deserved," Max said and folded his arms. "After all, he was the agent that was passing information to Brain Bender. I believe he was the one who loaded out that warehouse last night."

"If so, how did he end up like this?" Pro wondered.

Max smiled. "Remember what I said about clearing up the loose ends? I believe his 'partners' decided that he was one. Somehow, they drugged him, then put him in there. The trip to Atlanta in the hot sun would have taken care of the rest."

Reynolds said, "I have to call for medical assistance."

"Sure," Max replied. "That's probably a good idea."

Reynolds also stepped outside, and that left Pro and Max alone in the dark container.

"You left him there until we got here?" Pro queried.

Max looked at her with a stern face. "It could have been Luther or Jamie in the box if we hadn't raided that place last night. And they would probably be dead."

"So would Stanton after a day in this container," Pro pointed out.

Max grinned. "I guess he should be grateful I had that tracker on him."

Chu and Reynolds came back into the container.

"Ambulance is on the way," Reynolds said.

"So is the DEA," Chu added. "Pity we can't catch the guys who ran the scam."

"Oh you can." Max raised his eyebrows. "I mean, if you want to."

"What!" Reynolds bellowed, his voice echoing in the confined space.

"They are right on the ship," Max commented.

"You mean they're passengers on the ship?" Chu asked.

"Actually, they're part of the crew," Max explained.

Reynolds stared at Max for a moment. "How did you—never mind!" He looked from Pro to Chu. "How can we catch them?"

"I can recognize them," Pro said. "I've been to their offices." She turned to her father. "Edward and Elena?"

"Which is not their real names. Also Miss Bentley; she was the receptionist."

Reynolds looked at Pro. "Okay, Detective Thompson, you're with me. Detective Chu, could you be here for the DEA and the ambulance?"

"I can," Tom responded.

Reynolds pointed at Max. "And keep an eye on this guy."

Pro and Reynolds headed out, as Max and Tom moved to the door.

They stood outside with the large door open. Finally, Chu cleared his throat. "Should we untie Stanton?"

"I'll have to open his handcuffs and get my tracker back," Max said. "But as far as the zip cords, let the EMTs do it. After all, we don't want him filing a complaint against us."

"He'd have to do it from jail," Chu pointed out.

"Let's hope so."

There was a commotion, so Max and Chu stepped away from the container so they could see the ship. Reynolds was barking orders, and he and his team of heavily armed men and women were going up the gangplank with Pro in the lead, her weapon in her hands but pointed at the ground.

"So how did you find out they were working on the ship?"

"It's what I would do," Max said.

"What?" Chu blurted. "You don't know if they are there?"

"I didn't say that. I saw them get on the ship right before I contacted you."

Chu exhaled loudly. "I forgot you met them at the book club."

"And I've been watching the pier since early this morning, once I realized this is where the signal was for Stanton, and then I checked to make sure the ship wasn't leaving until late afternoon."

Sirens could be heard in the distance and growing closer, and with a nod, Chu headed out to the parking lot to meet the ambulance.

Max just smiled and leaned against the container.

* * *

Hours later, Stanton had been taken away on a stretcher by EMTs. Reynolds, Pro, and the team had three prisoners, and the Drug Enforcement Agency came in to claim jurisdiction.

Soon after the ambulance arrived, the media got wind of the bust and reporters were arriving while helicopters filled the sky to get video of the scene.

Pro was surprised that Max didn't move to the cameras like a moth to the flame, but the older man was subdued and stayed in the background as the drama unfolded. He stood, playing with the pair of high-security handcuffs he had taken off Stanton.

Once things were sorted out, the proper people were put in place to make sure the container full of drugs remained where it stood and did not get loaded aboard the ship.

As the lot cleared out and the ship prepared to leave, Pro and Chu got in their unmarked police car to return to the Midtown North Precinct.

Max approached them. "Is it okay for me to leave?"

"What happened to your van?" Pro asked.

"I parked it up the street so I could watch the pier, but not be in the way," Max explained.

"You're free to go, Max, but I want you to write up your eyewitness account of what happened," Chu commanded.

"Only one thing troubles me," Pro worried. "We still don't know who killed May Johnson and Thomas James."

"Oh, that. It was Stanton."

"Stanton? That stocky guy who is only about five feet five?" Chu frowned. "I don't buy it."

"You mean the man who was a Navy seal and is an expert with a knife and trained to break necks with his bare hands?"

"How do you know that?" Chu pressed.

"Stanton was always wearing that gold eagle pin on his lapel. That eagle is holding a trident and a flintlock. It's the pin awarded to members of a SEAL team. Plus, I think if you'll examine Stanton's black jacket, the one he was wearing the day he met us? There was a small tear in the back. I think it will match the fabric we found caught in the windowsill of May Johnson's apartment."

Chu shook his head. "I wonder what made him go rogue?"

"Greed?" Pro proposed.

"And I think pride," Max contemplated. "I think he busted so many drug dealers over the years that a part of him wanted to see if there was a way to import drugs that was undetectable."

"That's weird," Pro decided.

"No less than a fireman who starts fires," Max responded. "Perhaps he thought he could close it down any time he wanted and be a hero."

"He killed two agents who worked with him."

"My thoughts are that Thomas James wanted to bust the scam, but in that case, Stanton couldn't be the hero. It must have made him furious."

Pro nodded. "Well, we need to get to Zelig and find out who ordered those gimmicked windows—"

"Which will be Stanton," Max replied. "Why do you think he had Zelig shut down?"

"So it looks like once we start questioning people, we'll be able to wrap up the entire case," Chu said.

"But we have to work with the 84th," Pro complained. "Max, couldn't you have arranged to bust them in our part of town?"

Max smirked. "I can't do everything, Pro."

* * *

For Pro, the rest of the day was spent with reports, requests for interrogations, and planning which prisoner would be under whose jurisdiction. The DEA wanted to run the entire operation, as Stanton undoubtedly would be a black eye to the agency. However, homicide was a much larger crime than bribery or corruption, so Pro pushed up her chain of command that Stanton be under their jurisdiction.

They did have a bargaining chip, as Max gave Pro and Chu the list of the drug dealers from the book club, and they offered it to the DEA as a conciliatory prize.

About five in the afternoon, Pro turned from her chair to see Jamie out at the main desk. There was a large backpack on the ground next to him. She rose and walked over.

"I was just about to call you, detective," the desk sergeant said.

"That's fine, sergeant," Pro said and looked at Jamie. "What are you doing here?"

"I'm leavin'," he said, and slapped the backpack. "Can we talk?"

Pro indicated the interview room, and Jamie grabbed his backpack and went in.

"Are you okay?" Pro worried as she stepped into the room. She was amazed that she was standing in front of him and didn't have the slightest twinge of desire for the red-haired man. Was she that fickle, or had her decision to pair bond with Luther, and the rather remarkable bonding they'd had, finally quieted her doubts?

"The DEA raided the place where I was stayin' this afternoon. They questioned me for hours and after takin' me statement, they tol' me my visa was being revoked."

"I'm sorry, Jamie," Pro said.

"No, it was all a scam. They wanted to blame everything on me if it went bad. They had no real interest in me or me book."

She put a hand on his shoulder. "Write the book anyway, Jamie."

"Really?"

"I think you should. And don't give up. I mean if my father could be a famous magician, you can as well."

"I wish I could've been there for ye, Pro."

"You can't, Jamie," Pro said. "But I do have someone who *will* be there."

He took her hand and kissed it. "Luther is a lucky man."

"I'll be sure to tell him so every day."

"Good bye, Pro."

"Safe journeys, Jamie."

He grabbed his backpack and headed out the door. Pro sat on the corner of the table and watched him go. A part of her felt nostalgic, recalling the times they'd been together. But she now was truly ready to move on.

As she headed for the door her phone rang. With a sigh she put it to her ear.

"Can you join us for dinner out tonight?" Max said.

"I'm working late, and I then have a date with Luther."

"Bring him as well!" Max said. "The restaurant is only a block from the precinct. Say, 7:30?"

"Max—"

"Please?" Max insisted, as he rattled off the name of a very nice restaurant nearby.

"I'll see if my partner will let me off," Pro agreed.

"Great, see you then."

Pro hung up the phone and returned to her desk.

Tom looked up at her. "I think we're moving everything to the District Attorney, so a night off would be nice."

Pro nodded and then made a realization. "You want the night off to be with Julie!"

A smug smile appeared on Tom's face. "Well, I did propose."

"That's right," Pro said and slapped herself on the head with the palm of her hand. "That's what Max is going to do."

"I think it's nice he wants you there."

"Probably to make sure Mom doesn't say 'no,'" Pro glowered.

* * *

Pro left the precinct after seven, and Luther was outside waiting for her. She had warned him about the possible proposal, and the big man was wearing a nice suit with a subtle tie.

"Whoa, I feel underdressed," Pro said and gave him a peck.

"You always look good, my love," he said in his deep voice.

"Am I your love?"

"Oh yeah."

She took his arm and they headed down the street. "I have to say you are one sexy looking man."

"I know."

"And modest, too," she quipped.

They arrived at the restaurant, and seeing the maître d' in his tuxedo made Pro's feeling of being underdressed worse. Once Pro said, "Martin," they were quickly led to a table in the corner where Max and Elisha were already seated. Elisha had her hands in her lap.

Max rose to shake Luther's hand and welcome them both.

As they sat Elisha said, "I was wondering why we had a table for four." She looked over at Luther. "Nice to see you again."

"Nice to see you, Mrs. Thompson," Luther said.

Pro was pleased that Luther was always so polite to her mother.

"Shall we order?" Max said with a nervous tone to his voice. Pro could see he was sweating.

"Max, the children just got here," Elisha chided. She then turned to Pro. "We ordered a bottle of wine."

"Is it a special occasion?" Luther asked.

Max looked nervously at the table. "Actually, it is," he finally said. "I have an important announcement to make."

Here it comes, Pro thought. And then, for a moment, she felt sorry for Max. What if her mother said no? She didn't think she would, but there was always the possibility.

"I've...um...decided to go back to work," Max finally blurted.

Luther gave a big smile. "You mean, you're going to have another show? Where, in Vegas?"

Pro frowned. She hadn't expected this at all.

"Um...no...actually, I want to go into another line of work," Max explained.

Pro and Luther exchanged a glance.

Pro spoke up. "What line of work are you talking about?"

Max put on a brave smile. "Today I filled out the paperwork to become a private investigator."

Pro's mouth fell open, and she looked at her mother, who merely gave a knowing smile.

"What? That's...crazy!" Pro sputtered.

"I don't know, Pro," Luther said. "I mean he's done pretty well from what you told me on other cases. Sounds like your father has a knack for it."

Pro stared daggers at her date. "You...support this insane idea?" She then glared at her mother. "And you, you think he should do this?"

"Honey, I think Luther's right. Max has a talent for this. He told me all about how he solved your case for you just today."

Now Pro glared at her father. "*You* solved the case?"

"Well, I had help," Max replied nonchalantly. "I mean, come on, Pro, I've helped in several cases. I figure my work with the NYPD could count towards my required three years' experience to get my license."

Pro looked from person to person. "None of you think this is insane?"

Luther leaned forward in his chair. "I'll do one better. Mr. Marvell, I'll arrange for you to meet with people in my company. We have an entire private investigation department, and I'm sure they would be delighted to bring on someone with your skills. You can gain the experience you need right there."

"Thanks, Luther," the older man beamed. "And just call me Max. After all, we might be working together."

Pro looked at the table shaking her head. "So now I'll run into you at *all* my cases?"

"No, pumpkin, just the ones I'm hired to pursue."

Pro glared at Max. "Don't call me that!"

"Oh, honey, calm down," Elisha said. "I think it's good for Max to find some new interests."

"This was not the announcement I expected," Pro said. "I mean, he got a ring...I thought he would—"

"Propose?" Elisha interrupted. "Oh, yes, he did that this afternoon."

She pulled her left hand from under the table and showed off the ring.

"Congratulations," Luther roared and reached across the table to shake Max's hand again.

"And I was surprised. I thought Max was going to get me some unwearable thing that screamed 'money,'" Elisha chatted. "And then I saw this ring, and I knew that Max really understood me."

Max smiled. "I knew you wanted something that you could wear at work."

Pro glared at her father in disbelief but fought the urge to tell her mother it had been her idea.

"Well, then we should have champagne. This calls for a celebration," Luther said.

"Max ordered it when we arrived," Elisha said.

And at that moment, there was a *pop* and a waiter approached to set champagne flutes in front of each of them and another waiter stepped up with the napkin-wrapped bottle and filled each glass.

As it was poured, Luther asked, "So will you be Mister and Missus Marvell, or Martin?"

"Definitely Martin," Elisha sighed. "I'll have to get all my identification changed yet again."

Luther held his glass aloft. "To the soon-to-be newlyweds."

They clinked glasses and each one took a sip.

Pro had to admit, her parents were giddy, and Max often touched her mother's hand, and they gave each other glances full of meaning and joy.

As dinner was served and Pro relaxed, she told the others of Tom Chu's proposal, and they toasted to her partner as well.

She looked over at Luther and couldn't stop smiling. She really was in love with this man, and the night ahead would be filled with proofs of that love.

Max looked over at the younger couple. "So your partner is getting married and we're getting married—"

"Again," Elisha added.

"What's in the cards for you two?"

Luther looked over at Pro with the corners of his mouth turned up.

Pro suddenly got the implication.

"What, us? No, no, nothing like that," Pro quickly declared, and then looked over at Luther with panic in her eyes. "I mean, you're not going to...I mean, you can't...I mean, is this a set up?"

Luther could not stop the loud laugh that came out of his mouth. "No, Pro, this isn't a 'set up.' But I must say, you rush into crime scenes without breaking a sweat, but someone mentions marriage and you look like a scared rabbit."

"I do not!" she bellowed, and then lowered her voice. "Okay maybe a little."

"Don't worry, Pro. If I'm thinking I want to propose, I'll give you some warning," Luther said and patted her hand.

"So, I guess I'll be seeing you on the job," Max said as he took another sip of the bubbly liquid.

Pro looked at her father, then her mother, then the man she loved, sighed and said, "Yeah, I guess that was bound to happen."

The End

Free Prequel

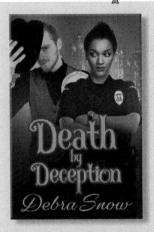

A street magician is murdered, a knife sticking from his chest. Can a NYPD rookie use her unique talents to find a killer?

Prophecy "Pro" Thompson is a female African-American, NYPD uniformed officer. Pro and her partner find a street performer stabbed through the heart and Pro decides to work the case in her free time.

During her investigation, Pro meets magician Jamie Tobin, a charming Irishman who tries to amaze her but becomes more interested in romancing her.

If you enjoy a kick-ass female protagonist, and a story mixed with crime, romance and comedy, you will love this fast-paced novella by Debra Snow.

This prequel takes places before Murder By Misdirection. Find out how the story begins!

http://www.debrasnow.com

About The Author

One night in 1979, I was in a club where a beautiful girl in a silver costume belly danced through the room. I approached her in the dressing room and begged to take classes with her.

Over the next ten years, I became a dancer, and started my own business. My performing life grew to include cruise ships, night clubs, resorts in the Poconos and Catskills, and TV appearances. I produced an audio tape and book series with Parade Records "Let's Belly Dance!"

In 1990, I auditioned at the Taj Mahal in Atlantic City and spent two years performing with the Taj Players. It was there I met my husband, Arjay Lewis. As our lives grew together, I began transitioning into teaching the dance, and found a fulfillment I never expected.

My husband has always been a writer, and when he started publishing, I became inspired to try my hand at the romantic mystery genre. This was a perfect complement to Arjay's paranormal mysteries.

Today we truly are, partners in crime...fiction

www.debrasnow.com

Made in the USA
Middletown, DE
14 February 2020

84528644R00161